After The Divorce

From Looking Back to Leaning In

Jeremy Stegall

To Paisley

Contents

CHAPTER 1

Good Morning

We are walking through a meadow, trails crisscrossing the prairie grass in the distance.

"Let's head to that overlook." We walk toward the cliff until we find ourselves standing above flowing water, holding hands, basking in our love. I take a deep breath, enjoying the sunshine and blue sky. The warmth of the sun kisses our exposed skin. I feel secure and connected, like I've always wanted to be.

"I love you, Joel," I hear, and I turn my attention from the water.

I smile brightly and sigh. "You know I've waited so long to hear those words. I love you too, babe," I say.

We stop walking, then hug and share a passionate kiss. A gentle breeze rolls over the grass. The contrasting temperature from the cool breeze and warm sun feels soothing.

"Joel, you know that we can't keep doing this," she continues. "We can't keep seeing each other this way. You have to find someone you can spend time with," she says, suddenly expressing concern.

"But I love you, and it feels like I've been looking for you forever. Can't we spend the day here?" I ask.

Out of nowhere, there's a loud crash, and I hear screaming. "What's that ringing?" I yell over the noise, covering my ears. All of a sudden, the cliff begins to crack and break away.

"Babe!" I scream. Then I wake up.

Just another dream.

I let out a deep sigh. I'm waking up alone; my wife, Angela, has already left for work. My phone has fallen off the nightstand and is under the bed, ringing. As I reach for it, I catch a glimpse of the time.

"I gotta get the hell out of here!" I yell, jumping out of bed. I begin rushing to get ready for work. Angie and our relationship can wait right now. It's six fifteen, and I should be at work already. My phone continues ringing, and I ignore the call, silencing the ringtone jamboree that is way too jarring so early in the day.

Anxious and tense, I frantically brush my teeth in the mirror. I haven't gotten a lot of sleep, and it shows.

"Why didn't my alarm go off an hour ago?" I say in frustration, attempting to remember the previous evening. All I recall are flashbacks of tense conversation and tears; I must have forgotten to set my alarm. Running downstairs to throw a bagel into the toaster, I quickly run back upstairs to throw on my work uniform.

"Damn it." I realize I also didn't do the laundry either, so I begin digging through the dirty laundry to find the shirt I meant to wash last night.

"Come on, Joel Edmonds. You've been the manager of a Hank and Harry's Hardware retail store for two months now. You should know better than to wake up late," I mutter to myself as I dig. My phone begins to ring again.

Who keeps calling me? "I swear, these spammers are relentless," I say as I dismiss the unfamiliar area code and phone number and turn the ringer to silent mode to help me concentrate. The phone continues to vibrate as I grab my bagel, rush out the door, and jump in my car. Getting to work is all I'm focused on. Rushing down Mills Civic Pkwy, I get onto I-35 South, toward Hwy 5. As I approach the city's south side, my phone rings again, and I finally pick up.

"Hello?" I answer with annoyance.

"Joel Edmonds, this is Thomas with Heartland Security Services. We're calling you because you're listed as the primary contact at Hank and Harry's Hardware on Veterans Memorial Parkway. We have been notified that your alarm has been going off for the last thirty-five minutes. There is a cruiser headed over there now," the dispatcher continues.

"Crap, really?" I say, now realizing my mistake. It's the security company I've been ignoring. It all began to make sense. They had been calling me and were the ones who jolted me awake. I must not have remembered to save their number in my phone.

Pulling into the strip mall parking lot, I see glass everywhere. Five of the seven stores in our corner of the parking lot have been vandalized. Driving around the glass on the ground, I park near the alley that leads to our employee parking behind the building. I immediately see the damage to the pet grooming shop across the alleyway.

"Wow, they got hit too," I say, looking at the barbershop and the dollar store. At least it's not just my store in this strip mall.

"Stores have been broken into before, but this appears to be some other inconsiderate asshole," yells the angry owner of South Side Pet Groomers, pacing back and forth in the parking lot as he speaks with a police officer.

I take a deep breath and get out of my car and begin to walk toward the front doors. The front doors are completely busted out, and there's glass everywhere. I put my head in my hands and start massaging my temples. I turn and walk toward the police officer.

"Pardon me, Lieutenant Freeman," I say, reading his name tag, "I'm the manager of Hank and Harry's Hardware. Do you know what happened?"

"Yeah." The officer responds without looking up from the notebook he's writing in. "Some juveniles, it looks like," he says, finally finishing his notation. "Kids throwing rocks at windows for a laugh or something."

"Wow."

"We'll be over in just a minute to get your statement," he continues. "We've done a perimeter check, and nothing seems out of place in the rear, but we haven't been inside yet. It doesn't look like they're still here or that they even entered any of the buildings. We can do a sweep for you to make sure no one's inside."

"Thank you, Lieutenant. I'd appreciate that," I say. "I'm glad to know I'm not going to be the first to enter the store."

There's always something going on over here, whether it's a beverage truck backing into the building or people getting arrested by the police for stealing from the dollar store next door. Just when you think it can't get any more ridiculous, it does.

After a few minutes, Lieutenant Freeman walks up with multiple officers, ready to enter the building. I go to unlock the door, quickly realizing that you can reach the lock with the glass now missing. Three officers head inside cautiously, ready to draw on anything that jumps out. Not the type of tension I'd expected to see before seven o'clock in the morning. At the same time, if the store is going to open late, it's better for this reason than because I overslept.

I walk over to the pet store, curious to see what I could of their damage. I'm immediately grateful that my storefront windows aren't busted like theirs, and it's just my front door that was damaged. Even with the police inside, I can't say I'm excited to go in. I looked at the clock on my phone and see that it's almost 7:00 a.m. exactly; already customers are starting to pull into the parking lot.

"What happened here?" I hear from behind me.

Turning around, I see my usual first customer of the day, Gil Roche, getting out of his busted-up contractors' van.

"I don't know yet," I call out. "I'm still trying to get inside and figure out what's going on. Give me a few minutes, and I'll put some coffee on. I can't even start sweeping up the glass until the cops finish their sweep of the store." I point at the broken glass.

"All right. Hurry up!" Roche says in a raspy voice. "I got a big order I want to put in, so make it quick," he says, chuckling, as if the chaos around him was no big deal. Even if the world was on fire and the sky was falling, he would still try to beat the heat and squeeze in another job.

As I'm talking to Roche, Lieutenant Freeman exits the store, giving me a thumbs-up that I'm OK to go in and open the store for the day. I hurry to the office and past multiple orders sitting in our delivery bay so I can look at the schedule to see who is coming in. My heart sinks when I realize that my right-hand man, Lucas, is off for the day, and my assistant will be starting in an hour.

"Oh, great," I say, and with perfect timing, both phone lines start ringing. "I can only do what I can do, right?" I dive right in and answer the first call.

Heading back up front, turning the lights on as I go, I notice glass on the ground by the coffeepot near the door. Even though the police have done their sweep, I realize I still need to check and make sure nothing has gone missing. Thankfully, at least I know no one's going to jump out from behind one of the shelving units to scare the crap out of me.

In between answering the phones and helping customers, I constantly have to announce, "Heads up, there's broken glass," as customers realize there's no glass in the front door. As I sweep up the glass, I notice four cars of potential customers and shake my head. I'm in the thick of it right now. It's getting busy, and I'm by myself.

Just then, another customer, Bart Honer, hands me a roll of duct tape.

"I saw the broken windows," he says. "You know I won't take no for an answer—I insist on helping you at least get some cardboard up to keep the cold air out. Maybe we can get this door covered up too, because this October air is kinda chilly and there's a breeze coming in," he says in his Midwestern accent.

Roche walks in, barking, "Is the coffee on yet?"

"Yeah, the coffee has been on," I say, pointing toward the coffeepot for customers.

"It looks like the coffee is out," Roche says with annoyance, and being an ass, he's testing my limits.

Just then my assistant manager, Kim, walks in. "Kim, put another pot of coffee on," Roche demands, holding up the empty coffeepot.

"No 'good morning' or 'how are you'?" Kim says, taking the pot from Roche.

I finish processing an order, and as I wheel it out from Will Call, I pass Kim. I can hear a lip-smacking sound that's generally used to show displeasure with someone.

It's true—there is tension between us. Yesterday, Kim "overslept" and was two hours late for her shift, and I was late to couples counseling because of it. Angie and I ended up arguing about my dirty uniform.

My part-timer, Patricia, had been here by herself and gotten bombarded with an afternoon surge of orders coming in. Every time I catch a glimpse of Kim, it appears she wants to say something to me. *Ugh. Why does she have to make everything so complicated?* I roll my eyes.

That makes two conversations I need to have today.

"You were thirty minutes late twice last week," I begin, walking over to the water fountain where Kim is taking her time filling the coffeepot.

"My phone didn't go off," she says, shrugging her shoulders. "Listen, I'm tired."

"Kim, I understand it can be difficult getting started in your first store as an assistant manager. It gets better, I can assure you. We all experience some degree of fatigue working in this industry. I still need you to get here on time."

"All right," she says, indicating zero interest in what I'm saying.

I put my hands up and step back. "What is that? Why the attitude?"

"Hey, y'all! What's going on?" George Martin, a loyal customer with Smart Renovations, walks in, interrupting our conversation.

As George walks up, I finish with Kim. "I won't say anything to HR about this, but please learn from this," I whisper.

I get a full lip-smack/eye-roll combo. "OK," Kim responds, walking out of the break room.

"Good morning, George," I say, walking over to greet my up-and-coming remodeling customer.

"Hey, Joel, I want to chat with you. I've got some things coming up, and there's something I want to talk to you about."

"Sure, we can chat in the office. Give me a second."

I rip a strip of duct tape with my teeth and head back to finish taping cardboard to the door with Bart.

****

It's been a few hours now, and I've got three people helping me inside. When I walk back inside, George is toiling around in the H&H Hardware Helper section, looking at one of the new products on display.

"You know, I just heard about these," he says, holding a paint touch-up kit. "I saw the guys on TV pitching their idea from a duct-taped handle to a can or something, and now, look at this. I could have done this," he says in playful frustration, shaking his head. "I've been in this industry for ten years now. I bet you these guys are millionaires, and here I am."

Then he catches himself. "Hey, by the way, I wanted to chat with you about something. Do you have a second?" he asks.

"Sure," I respond, and we make our way over to the office.

"Can we close the door?" he asks.

"Sure—have a seat," I respond, confused.

"Listen, man. I like you, and I want to let you know that your assistant is using disrespectful language toward the customers and not completing orders when you're not here. I don't know what you've heard, but Roche called her a dumbass under his breath a couple of days ago. I was standing by the cabinet fixtures, and I'm sure she heard pretty clearly what he said," he begins.

"Yeah," I say, shaking my head. "I've noticed a few orders left unfinished." I rub my head. "I can assure you that it's not going to impact how we take care of you and your business." I shift my position in my chair. "Everyone experiences hiccups when they're new. I'm sure when you were new, you had to learn a few things too, right? Didn't your old man want to chase you off at a jobsite or two?" I asked jokingly.

I've known George Martin for about five years at this point, and joking with him was common.

"Let me tell you a story about the first time my old man sent me out of state alone with a crew," he starts off. "I was twenty-five, old enough to know better, and I got into it with some store manager in Missouri. I was in a pinch," he says looking up and leaning back in his chair, "trying to finish using this waterproofing stuff for a roofing job at a new hotel. To prove a point about how big a deal I was, I said I would knock every gallon of paint in that store off the shelves if they didn't get me what I needed and in a reasonable time frame. I did knock off a couple of gallons, too, and they chased me out of the store!"

"Really?" I ask, shocked to hear this new story.

George often would say stuff like this, but I'm never sure if I can believe his stories. But if he's giving me a heads-up that someone is slipping up in the store, I can trust his word and at least investigate.

"What a bitch of a day for all of this to happen! I'm running on a bagel and a half cup of coffee," I say.

The store phone in my pocket begins ringing. "Hold on, George," I say, pausing to answer.

"Hank and Harry's, this is Joel. How can I help you?"

An upset voice begins yelling, "Kimberly Miller is not fit for her position!"

Immediately taken aback, I respond, "Who is this?"

"Junior Martin! Can't you tell my voice by now?"

"Why are you yelling, Junior?" I ask calmly. It sounds like he's driving with the windows down.

"I don't want to shop anywhere else, and I will get even more pissed if I have to continue to let you know when another order is missing or forgotten!" he continues.

"What are you talking about?"

"Kim said she was going to leave a note in the office with my order written on it. You were missing some products, she said, and she was going to leave a note for you," Junior explains. "When will you have the order ready?" he says in a frustrated tone. He's not in a joking mood like his father.

"Listen, we still don't have the material," I say. "I'm standing here with your dad right now. We'll take care of this, I promise."

"Let me know soon as you can, Joel. And don't let my dad forget to place the order for the Git N Go we're starting," he says, hanging up.

"Hey, George, I've got to talk to Kim about something Junior said about an order. Can we revisit this conversation later?" I ask.

"Sure, Joel. One last thing," he says, and my heart drops. "We got the bid for remodeling the Git N Go grocery store, and I'll need to get my first order placed here soon."

"Sure thing, George," I say. "That was Junior, and he's pissed." I begin rubbing my head again and then stand up. "We'll get that order placed, George." As we leave the office and walk past the break room, I notice Kim and enter, saying, "I need to speak with you." Before I get another sentence out of my mouth, Kim is ready to argue.

"I won't be disrespected," she begins. "I left you a sticky note saying that we didn't have material for Smart Renovations, and I was going to come in and figure out how to get it. You didn't even give me a chance to do that before blaming me for the order not being done, and you didn't even acknowledge the fact that I put a sticky note on your desk," she begins, quickly raising her voice in frustration and agitation. "You are a wolf in sheep's clothing! And you are not doing your job as a store manager, Joel!" she says with an attitude.

I could feel the hair standing up on my arms. "I haven't even said anything about an order," I begin. "What is going on?"

"You act like you can do all of this by yourself, and I'm tired. I'm gonna make you figure out how you're gonna do this all by yourself and keep coming in late because you're doing a shitty job with the schedule, and you're not being consistent," she continues.

"What?" I ask, trying to follow her conversation. *Sticky Note? Inconsistent?* "Kim, the front door is missing glass, we've got a store full of people, and I'm getting yelled at by Junior Martin over an order he gave you. Are you kidding me?" I didn't notice that I was beginning to shout. I feel the anger and tension from all the stress bubbling to the surface, and I'm barely able to keep it in.

"Listen, can we talk about your note later?" I ask. "There's a lot going on and a line is starting to back up in front. I need your help. Your sticky note is not a big deal."

"Whatever," Kim says, and turns to walk toward the front registers to help out with the logjam of customers.

I look at my watch; it's eleven thirty. *How the heck did it get to this point in the day already?* I take a deep breath. I barely have enough staff in the store to handle all the customers, and I notice I might have to jump on a register. As I begin walking toward the registers, once again the phone in my pocket begins to ring, and I answer.

"Hey, Joel, it's John." John is my district manager.

"Oh, hey, John," I say, and head toward the office.

"Hey, how's it going? I thought I would've heard from you by now," he begins. "Is everything OK over there?"

"Hey, yeah, uh, it's been a busy morning over here. There's been a break-in at the store. I spoke with the police and filed an incident report, and they did a sweep of the premises. They're guessing juvenile vandals," I respond. "Outside of that, nothing is missing or damaged other than the front doors." I ramble on. "Kim was late again, and we got into it again. And I got a couple of complaints about her from customers today." I notice from the office doorway that there's an even worse buildup of customers in Kim's line. "Ugh, can I call you back?" I ask. "There's a logjam of people up front."

"Well, I want to make sure nothing is damaged," John says, trying to continue the conversation. "Do you need me to call HR? What did Kim say?"

"I assure you, John, the store is in good hands. I just see lines backing up, and Kim is fumbling around with her computer. I'll give you a call in about an hour, OK?" I say, clearly in a hurry.

"OK. Call me back," John responds, and we hang up.

At least I mentioned the assistant manager argument. *Damn it.* The lines are backing up. I'm going to have to help out with the logjam at the registers. I see that Kim is confused and trying to figure out a problem with her computer while grumbling customers in her line are becoming frustrated by a series of worsening issues.

Before I can leave the office, Kevin Ashland, our store's supporting sales rep, walks in.

"Hey, Joel, whataya know, kid?" he says, greeting me. For whatever reason, he's always called me "kid" ever since I became his assistant manager a couple years ago, back when he managed this store. When he became a sales rep, the nickname stuck with me, even though I'm now the manager and in my thirties.

"Man, I can't even begin to tell you right now," I say. "The lines are backing up, though, and I want to jump in and help out the crew."

"Ah, they can handle it," he says waving his hand nonchalantly." Besides, this is how they gain experience and develop character." Noticing the stress on my face, Kevin changes his tone. "Are you OK? I noticed the cardboard on the door, and the parking lot looks like this place is a crime scene."

Just then, Kim walks in, begins shuffling things around on her desk, grabs something, then walks out of the office.

"How are things going in the store?" Kevin asks, noticing the tension.

"Pretty brutal. George Martin gave me a heads-up that some things were starting to slip, and Junior called this morning and gave me an earful too," I say. "Why do you ask?"

"George is considering shopping at Hank and Harry's on the West Side because of some issues with Kim over the last month. Lucas also told him he didn't like her attitude and wasn't going to deal with her much longer."

I let out a loud sigh and roll my eyes. "What am I going do?" I say in frustration. "I'm only one-third of the way through my day, and it doesn't feel like today is going to get any easier."

"Hey, listen," Kevin says, "I'll hang out here for a couple of hours today and help out. I can already see you're stressed and frazzled, and I know your marriage has been weighing on you. Take a load off, man. I'm here." He puts his arm around me.

"Thanks, man." I take a deep breath. "I appreciate your help." I feel my eyes start to tear up.

CHAPTER 2

The Happy Life

I arrive home around six o'clock, the blue sky well into becoming a shade of orange with the setting sun. I would've preferred stopping to rake all the leaves that have blown into the yard, but as the garage doors open, I can see Angela pacing back and forth in the kitchen, trying to calm herself.

Before she notices me, she throws her hands in the air. Her body language indicates to me that this day is not over.

As I walk into the kitchen, I'm right in the midst of yet another argument.

"It's like, two years have gone by, and things aren't changing," she says.

"Hey. Give me a second. I'm barely in the door. You know, it would nice if you said, 'Hello, honey,' and gave me a hug instead of jumping on me like this. What the hell?"

"Listen, we need to talk, and we need to talk now," she continues. "I keep going back and forth on why this is such a hard thing for you to understand. I'm asking you to stop spending money and be responsible. You spent money on hockey tickets, and we don't need this! Not asking me about it is not cool. We need to save for retirement and start putting more money in the bank now."

"I understand that we need to be responsible," I say. "We *are* saving money. These tickets are important to me, and I thought you wouldn't mind. It's not like I'm irresponsible."

Of course, Angela does have a point. I didn't think before I committed us to season tickets for the Iowa Grizzlies hockey team. I haven't put a lot of thought into anything beyond what I wanted. Saving money was never a conversation I'd taken seriously.

"Listen, babe. I'm willing to work within the budget. But I need to be able to live. I just can't go to work and come home and sit in the corner. I need to do something to alleviate stress."

"Stress? *I'm* stressed! We're not putting any money in the bank, and you said that you were going to put five hundred dollars in our account last week. Did you do it? No! You didn't do it. You spent it on those tickets!" she says in frustration, throwing her hands in the air.

"Well, you're always talking about how much money you're saving, which sounds a lot to me like you're spending money, too," I say in defense. "Even if you're saving money when you're buying stuff at a discount. "

"I'm decorating the house! Making this place a home for us," she retorts.

"We have three clocks in the living room. Two are on the same wall, and one is just decorative," I argue, pointing to the clocks in the family room. "You keep getting on me about the one thing I spend money on. I thought it'd be fun for us to do together," I say, shrugging my shoulders.

"Well, I'd appreciate being consulted," Angela responds.

"I thought that it would be a good time and something cool for us to do. Do you really want me to consult you for every decision?" I ask.

"Yes," she says without pause.

"Yes? Really?" I say in disbelief.

"Yes, and we also have other things to talk about too. Don't you remember calling me fat last night?" she says, her eyes wide and her nostrils flaring.

"I didn't call you fat," I respond, shaking my head. "I noticed that you've stopped exercising and asked you about running a half marathon this year with me. You barely want to get out of bed or do anything active anymore," I say.

I sit on the couch, beginning to tear up. "Angie, it's been a very crappy day today. Someone broke into the store this morning, and Kim yelled at me while we had a store full of people."

Angie looked down and began fidgeting with her ring. "Oh, I just don't know," she responds under her breath.

"Don't know what?" I ask. "I'm not freaking out on you about the things you stopped doing once we got married. I told you—it's been a rough day."

"We need to find ways to save money, Joel. I like the clocks, and I think they're a good idea, and I've still got to finish decorating all the rooms," she continues, walking into the kitchen.

"I want something for us to do together that's a fun experience," I say. "And I am putting money into my retirement. What's wrong with that?" As soon as those words came out of my mouth, I regretted bringing up the subject of retirement.

"That's not enough! We'll never hit our financial goals," she says in frustration, coming back into the room.

"I don't even know what that is—'our goals,' " I say, making air quotes. "Did I miss something?"

"You have no money, Joel," Angela says, starting to cry. "If you're ever going to retire, I'm just asking you to prioritize this for a few years."

"What type of man are you expecting me to be? A homebody?" I say, following her back into the kitchen.

"I want a man that's going to take me out and has money in the bank," Angela says, crossing her arms. "I want us to have nice things. But not right now. You just got promoted and got a raise. You have to start putting more money into your retirement account, and some money needs to go into the bank."

I walk past Angela out of the room. "All I wanted was a hug after this shitty day, but if this is what you want—happy wife, happy life, right?—I'll put money in our savings account next paycheck."

I make my way upstairs and take off my work uniform with today's added dirt and sweat. *What about me and what I want? We're always doing what she wants. When she asks for my suggestion, it either doesn't sound like fun, or she doesn't want to do it.*

Our trip to LA a couple of months ago was the first step in our relationship recovery, getting out of town together. At that point, we didn't have much to say to each other and just hung out at sports bars, trying to make small talk. You could see that the walls were going up.

Why can't I do what I'm doing? Don't I matter in this relationship? What about give-and-take and working together? I'm saving money, and I have gotten a promotion. It feels like if I don't jump when Angela says something or follow her strategy, I'm the asshole. Is this what marriage is? Every day we wake up a mile apart from each other in bed, not feeling any connection physically. If I don't follow her rules, then something is wrong, and I'm the problem? Maybe I need to get out of this house and focus on just getting the store in order.

Angela walks in and sits on the bed. "I'm sorry, Joel. I just think our financial security is really important."

"Angela, I don't know about you, but I'm not happy right now. I don't feel like what I want matters or that you even care," I say, closing my eyes.

"Joel, sometimes you don't get what you want, even if you can afford it," she says crossing her arms.

"We keep going in circles. Over and over again, arguing about each other's tendencies to spend 'our money,'" I say, making air quotes with my hands. "Where is any physical intimacy? What I want doesn't matter. You only want the future you demand to see. Retirement, whatever. You always get what you want," I begin tearing up. As tears begin falling, my body begins to go numb. *Maybe she's right.*

"You know, Joel," she says, sobbing through her own tears, "if I were any other woman, I would have said that I have a problem with the size of this diamond you gave me. But I'm not most girls, so I won't say anything." Slowly removing her wedding ring from her finger and throwing it at me, she says, "You need to demonstrate your commitment to this relationship and this ring. Prove you're serious about being in this marriage."

"Prove that I'm serious about being in this marriage?" I say, trying to catch the ring as it bounces off my chest. I hadn't even considered taking off my ring.

"I put serious, sentimental thought into this," I say, looking down at the ring. It was a custom design from Paxton's Jewelry, and my grandmother passed down the diamonds from her wedding ring, which had been passed down to her. It wasn't just a ring I got hit with. It was a painful blow.

I put my head in my hands and start to sob uncontrollably.

"I'm going to bed. I need you to leave this room," Angela says, gesturing toward the door, kicking me out of our bedroom with the same cold, emotionless stare that followed my infrequent requests to have sex.

I can't stay in this house.

Presley, our puppy, follows me. We'd rescued her earlier this year, and she was now the one ray of sunshine in our relationship. I didn't want to name a dog Presley, but Angie would jokingly sing about hound dogs and how Presley was a friend of hers, so, once again, happy wife, happy life. Even though Presley was a black-and-white Labrador, the name stuck.

I walk down the stairs, back into the family room, and over to the window. I can't see the trees now, but I know it looks like a forest of green during the day. Tears begin welling up again. For the first time, I am ready to admit out loud that divorce is likely.

It's hard to believe that it was only one o'clock yesterday morning when Angie dropped a bombshell on me, saying she wanted to take a break from talking every day and wasn't sure she would be going on the upcoming trip to Florida we had been planning.

Looking out the window, I remember the first night we were in this house. We were dreaming about bedrooms where kids clearly chose the bedroom colors: one, Celtics green; the other, hot pink and purple. We were talking about the future and sharing bottles of wine. We were so excited. Our first home together, where we were going to raise a family.

At thirty-three years old, I'm married, I have a house and a dog and tickets to the Iowa Grizzlies. Granted, I am in trouble for deciding to get them. I've heard the advice about asking for forgiveness versus permission at the beginning of the relationship, and I figured it was a gamble that could pay off. Angie and I could have date nights, and I could take customers and employees from the store and write off the tickets. Deep down, I really want the tickets for myself.

I'm not happy. What does a life of fulfillment even look like? There are things that I want too. At least little five-month-old Presley is here to console me, curled up and sleeping peacefully in her bed.

Maybe I could stay at Evan's house over the weekend. How much can one person take?

As I walk around the house in my favorite fleece that Angie gave me, I tense up, thinking, *I'm not giving this sweater back. I've probably got enough tears on it to call it my own by now.* Walking into the kitchen, I remember the bottles of vodka in the cupboard left over from the last football tailgate. *I'm not in the mood to get drunk. That's not going to solve my problem.*

I go upstairs to the spare bedroom. *It's been such a long day.* I'm trying not to be sad, but I am. I have no clue what's going to happen.

As I lay in bed, my mind continues to replay our arguments over and over.

"Joel, I shouldn't have married you," I imagine Angela saying. *Maybe we got married too soon? There were plenty of flags.*

Maybe there was more I could've said when I had the chance. If only I could've seen it; if only I was paying attention at first. I have my issues to work through and a deep desire to be accepted for who I am. Who doesn't want to be themselves and be accepted?

"Joel, you get up and go to work and do what you need to. You get married, you buy a house with a fence on the hill," I recall being told. I began to tear up again, eventually falling asleep.

❋❋❋

Waking up to my alarm, I jump out of bed, forgetting it's Saturday. "Whew!" I sigh loudly.

Today isn't just any Saturday, though; it is my last Saturday in this house. I slowly open the door to peek across the hallway to see if Angie is awake and notice that the door is open and she is gone. All the better. I don't want to see her right now anyway. I quickly pack a couple of suitcases with my clothes, I get Presley's dog food and supplies together, and I jump in my car. Heading to Waukee, I'll be staying with my friends Evan and Mel for a few days.

When I arrive at Evan's house, he immediately asks, "You want a bloody Mary?"

"It's 8:00 a.m., man," I respond, getting out of the car.

"Yeah, so? This is a special occasion," Evan says, giving me a hug. "Mel and I are happy to have you here."

It's been a few months since I've seen them. In fact, the last time we were together, Angela made a drunken and unfounded accusation of infidelity between Melanie and me, introducing a weird vibe into our friendship. I've known Evan and Melanie since college, and they are like family to me. They've always offered anyone needing refuge a place to stay.

"Sure, I'll have one," I say, succumbing to the temptation. "Thanks, man."

"So, how are ya doing?" Evan asks as we walk inside.

"I keep having repeating thoughts about the relationship," I begin, setting my bags down and taking Presley off of her leash. "How do I create a life I'd feel happier about now? I feel like we rushed into the wedding. Everyone was getting married, you know?" I take a seat at the kitchen counter.

"Yeah," Evan says as he hands me a drink decorated with a pickle, sausage stick, and two well-balanced olives. "There were a few years there when we all got married."

"Four weddings in three years!" I exclaim. "I was getting close to thirty, and it felt like it was my turn," I say, taking a sip. "Damn, man. This is delicious!"

"Thanks man. I've gotten better at making them since the last time you were here," Evan says, smiling and nodding, then sipping his drink.

"Angie is saying again that I don't save enough for retirement and need to take ownership of my decisions. It's been a miserable couple of years."

"Yeah? It can feel like it sucks sometimes. I thought you two were trying to make it work. You did take that trip to LA," Evan says.

"She doesn't want to go on the trip to Florida we've been planning," I say in frustration. "I'm still going. I paid for the tickets already."

"Damn, man. Well, you tried," Evan says with a shrug.

"I'd never imagined that she would be one person before we were married, then do a 180-degree turn and expect me not to have feelings about that," I say, stirring my drink with the pickle, then taking a bite.

"All you can do is continue to live the best you can while it sucks and you're trying to figure it out," Evan says. "How are things at the store?"

"Ha!" I say with a laugh. "We were broken into yesterday, and my assistant manager showed up late and called me a wolf in sheep's clothing."

Just then, from down the hall, Melanie interrupts. "OK, Joel, I'll be ready to hear everything in a minute." She walks in, brushing her teeth.

Sitting at the custom hardwood kitchen table she and Evan just purchased, Melanie joins us, bringing their border collie, Bower, into the room. Bower and Presley immediately begin sniffing each other and start roughing around, so we put them outside.

"How are you, Joel?" Melanie asks.

"Well, I can't say I didn't see this coming, the more I think about it. There were warning signs and flags that I ignored," I begin. "Drinking and a 180-degree personality change is only part of it. I don't know how we got to where we are now," I say, blaming Angela and taking no responsibility for what I said or how it impacted our misunderstandings.

"Have you put any thought into piecing that together?" Melanie asked.

"No," I respond. "It was awesome tailgating. We even had mutual connections that we didn't recognize until we started dating. It almost felt like it was serendipitous and meant to be. I figured why not? We were having such a good time."

"Yeah, it is kind of weird that you went to the same university but never saw her on campus or at any hockey games," Melanie says.

"Right," Evan chimes in. "You'd think we would've seen her in the student section at the games we went to, or afterward."

"Yeah, meeting her online after graduation and finding out that we lived across the street from each other felt like the stars were lining up. It was a great time going back to Ames to see old friends and tailgate," I say.

"Do you think that was a problem?" Melanie asks.

"For a while, it was all good, but it seems like it was becoming more about drinking. I was only there for the social aspect," I say in response.

"You got along with her friends and her family," Evan says, pointing out that things weren't all as bad as I was recalling.

"Yeah," I say with a sigh. "I felt like I was bonding with everyone, and they were very welcoming. A few weeks ago, I made a comment to one of her friends about how the relationship wasn't going so well. I was drunk, but her response was such a shock. She said she didn't want to hear what I was saying. That started to sour me on drinking so much. Like I wasn't able to keep a lid on things," I admit with shame.

A wave of sadness comes over me, and I begin to tear up.

"I think I wanted something different than being married," I continue.

"It's not like all of your drinking experiences together were bad," Evan says in response. "Do you remember when Mel and I first met Angela at our bar crawl downtown?"

"Yeah, we had those matching tank tops. I liked those," Melanie chimes in.

"That was a good idea. It was so much fun going out and dancing," I say, recalling the bar crawls we used to do in our late twenties.

"It was fun hanging out with everyone and running around the city," Evan says.

"At the end of that night, when everyone was going to Charlie's to start the dance-off, Angie and I made a stop at a hot dog stand. I remember holding her hand, and I had a feeling like 'I think I love this girl.' She caught my eye right when I had the thought and asked me what I was thinking. I couldn't hold it in and responded, 'Baby, I'm thinking about you. I think I love you.'

"She nervously responded, 'Yeah?'—and gave this smile. It was a beautiful moment, my favorite of the night. We met you both upstairs not too long after that." I start to smile a little, remembering that day.

"I didn't know what happened to you that night," Melanie says. "I was so busy trying to calculate the final score of who won. You guys were all about the final score that night."

"That night was a mess," Evan says, chuckling.

"The night she called the cops when I was at the bar down the street was a breaking point. The warning signs were becoming more consistent, and it felt like things were way off. She'd been at happy hour after work, and I was out trying to make new connections after I got promoted. At the networking event, she couldn't get a hold of me, so she started calling you, intoxicated and accusing you of covering up my having an affair," I say, tearing up again. My joy has been short-lived, and I fall back into the negative and recall another memory.

"The demand for a 'happy wife, happy life' was becoming a passive-aggressive demand to follow the rules set by her and hold the values she had grown up with," I explain.

Evan and Mel sit at the table in silence, listening intently to my confessional. "I'm not happy with my life," I say, letting out a deep sigh.

"Just two weeks ago, I was sitting in my back warehouse, my assistant Kim had called off, and I had to work open to close. The last customer of the day was the girlfriend of a critical customer and threw a tantrum about a discount that didn't apply to them. She was demanding a better price for some gallons of paint five minutes before the end of a thirteen-hour day. Whether at the store or at home, I'm dealing with something challenging. Is this what life is meant to be when you get promoted and get married?" I ask. "I have an assistant manager that won't listen, and a wife that wants to be in charge of where I go and how I live."

"Have you thought about getting help or seeing a therapist?" Melanie asks.

"No, not really," I say.

"How can you improve your relationship if you don't have help or support?" Mel asks gently.

"Or get people to follow my direction in the store? I'm struggling to get Kim to listen to me," I say, posing another challenge I perceive.

I've had enough talking about Angie and the good old days. We were supposed to visit my friend Andre in Florida for a few days and another relationship recovery vacation. Andre was part of my wedding party, and we played hockey together in high school before heading off to college.

"I'm going to call my buddy Andre in Florida and let him know about the change in our plans."

Looking out the glass patio doors, I can see Presley and Bower both lying in the backyard, tongues hanging out and panting, their wrestling match on pause for a few moments to catch their breath. I walk outside, closing the door behind me, and call Andre.

"Hello?" I hear Andre's deep voice on the other end of the phone after a few rings.

"Hey, Andre, it's Joel. I . . . um . . . wanted to give you a heads-up. Angie won't be coming with me to Florida. I'll be coming down alone. It looks like we've gotten to the breaking point."

"Aw, man, I'm sorry to hear that," he responds.

"Leaving Iowa could be a good thing to help me figure out my next steps. Are you cool if I still come down solo?" I ask.

Andre responds, "I can throw some things together, and we can make this a good time—like a recovery vacation for you. We can grab tickets to a hockey game down here, and I've got a buddy with a boat. We can tweak a few things and spend time together."

"Sounds good, man," I say. "I could go for a good time right now."

CHAPTER 3

Sunny Moments

"It's been good having you here this past week, Joel," Evan says as he arrives home after work. "How are you feeling now?"

"Yeah, I know I've been keeping quiet," I say somberly. "I'm starting to figure out which end is up. I had a conversation with a coworker a couple of days ago, and he recommended a lawyer I could talk to—Gordon Merrick. I'm going to give him a call to see if he can help me out with the divorce."

"Nice. I bet that's got to be expensive," Mel says.

"I'm working on figuring that out," I say. "So far, it looks like about a grand."

"Well, that's not too bad," Evan says, sounding reassuring. "What are your thoughts about your living situation?"

"I have to move out of the house. There's no way I can stay there. Who knows what the hell has been going on over there since I've been gone. I'm not looking forward to going back and telling Angela about having spoken with the lawyer," I answer.

"If it helps at all, you can stay here until you get some money saved for an apartment," Evan says. *He's so kind to offer to help,* I think gratefully.

"Thanks. Most of the money I have is in a joint bank account with Angela, and I don't know how she'll be if I try to get any of it out. I bet it'd be a headache because of how she is about saving and what

I put into it versus what she has. I don't want to argue about money with her again," I explain.

"Well, stay as long as you need, man. We've got a spare room for you," Evan says.

"Thanks. Maybe I could stay here for a couple of months? I have just enough in my savings to cover the lawyer. I'll need to save for a deposit on an apartment. I can contribute to the food while I'm here," I say.

"No, man, don't worry about it. Talk to the lawyer and get your ducks in a row. Figure out what you need," Evan insists.

"Thanks—it's a weight off my shoulders and one less thing to worry about now." I pull out my phone to see what time it is. Tuesday, 4:25 p.m. The delay in calling the lawyer can't wait any longer after making this arrangement.

"I'm going to go call the lawyer to schedule a consultation," I say, getting up from the couch and walking back to the guest bedroom for privacy. I nervously dial the number, and the phone starts to ring. I'm sweating.

"Hello? Gordon Merrick's office," I hear on the other end.

"Is this Gordon Merrick of Merrick and Associates?" I begin. "I was referred to you by an acquaintance of yours, Kevin Ashland. I'm thinking of filing for divorce—well, I guess I am, because I'm calling you."

I chuckle nervously and take a breath, trying to get it together. "I'm currently separated from my spouse, and I need representation to help with my divorce proceedings. Is that something you can help me with?"

"Yeah, I know Kevin Ashland. We go way back," Gordon says. *Whew, so far, a good response.* "We met when his wife was in law school, and they were still dating. Tell me more about your situation."

"We've been together for three years now," I begin. "No kids. We have a house and a joint savings account. Things are, uh . . . I'm not happy."

"No kids? Lucky man," Gordon says, sounding surprised. "That could've been a nasty issue for you. Sometimes those proceedings drag out for a long time, and they get expensive," he explains. "How are things between the two of you? Are you able to speak to each other?"

"I don't know if I want to be in the room with her," I say. "Do I have to be?"

"No, we can schedule times for the two of you to come by separately to sign the paperwork. The fee is $1,200. Why don't we get you on the schedule to come in, and we'll have you start the process and sign a few papers? Then we can talk more about the timeline. Divorce is more common than you might think. Come in, and we'll talk about what needs to happen for things to be finalized. We'll make sure you get your i's dotted and t's crossed."

"Thanks, Gordon. I appreciate it," I say, trying to smile.

"No problem. I look forward to meeting you. These are unfortunate circumstances, don't get me wrong, but you'll get through this," he says before transferring me to his receptionist to schedule an in-person appointment.

The next step: break the news to Angela.

***

As I slowly approach the driveway, I reach for the garage door opener, noticing I'm sweating again. If there's any moment I have not been looking forward to, it's this moment—telling Angela that I want a divorce.

I park my car and go inside. The TV is on, but Angela isn't around. I walk upstairs and down the hall to the bedroom. *Where is she?* I walk down to the sewing room in the basement—she's not there either. I put my hands on my hips, confused. Then I notice that she's outside, sitting on the deck and looking out at the view.

"Hey," I say in almost a whisper as I walk outside.

"Hey," Angela says, not turning around.

"How are you?" I ask, feeling completely awkward.

"Good," Angela says calmly. "What have you decided?"

I take a deep sigh and fidget a little. "OK, I guess there's no sugarcoating this," I say. "Angela, this isn't a decision I'm making easily here. After spending some time at Evan and Mel's, reflecting on what we've gone through and the issues we have, I think it might be best if we end things here."

"There are things that I'm not happy with, and every time I open my mouth to try to share with you what I'm struggling with, we end up in an argument," I continue. "Then comes the defensiveness and all the back-and-forth. Everyone at the wedding said the first couple of years would be the best years of our lives. I don't know about you, but I've been miserable."

Angela turns around. Crossing her arms, she rolls her eyes at me and starts to tap her foot. "Is there anything I could've done different?" she asks with a straight face.

I knew deep down there were things, but this was the same tactic that always opened me up for the next go-around. I take a deep breath and brace myself. "It's this attitude when you ask me what's wrong—when I open up to you, you attack me. This isn't a game. I'm trying to take care of myself." I throw my hands in the air, at a loss. "I feel like I can't be who I am. Like I'm some controlled puppet who has to do things the way you do. I'm the problem. 'Happy wife, happy life' doesn't mean that what I want doesn't matter, Angela."

"Well, these are the choices you have to make," she says in response.

"It's . . . it's like I don't know who you are or what the heck is going on here. You were one person before we got married, and now you're in a perpetual state of nothing's good enough. I'm not living that way for the rest of my life. I don't know if I want to go into it again. I spoke to Gordon Merrick, the divorce attorney, earlier and scheduled a meeting with him next week about finalizing the details for divorce."

Angie starts to tear up. Her bottom lip is shaking. She asks, "If you've already talked to a lawyer, what's the next step?" She's definitely pissed now. Her eyes hold mine in a piercing stare.

"I'm, sorry . . . I . . . this isn't what I wanted," I stammer.

"Whatever. Give me his number. I'll call him if that's what you want. This really hurts, Joel," she continues, revealing the first crack in her armor. "I'm very disappointed in you. This is so embarrassing for me. Everything that my family did to help us get us into this house . . . I can't believe you would do this. I'm so upset with you. I need you to leave."

I take a deep breath.

She begins wiping away the tears with her sleeve. Her face is turning red. Presley circles her ankles, trying excitedly to lick her. Angela bends down and begins petting her. She starts crying in earnest. "I guess you're taking her too?" she asks, with more emotion than the death stare I just got.

"You know how much I've always wanted a dog," I say. "You can have the house and the money in the bank. Just let me take the dog."

Angela looks down at Presley, still crying, and gives her a big hug.

"I need you to leave," she says again, trying to regain her composure.

"I'm grabbing a few things first, and then I'll head back to Evan's. I'll be back this weekend to get the rest of my stuff," I say, walking into the house.

"Fine," Angela says as I go inside and head upstairs.

Those were the last words we would ever say to each other.

* * *

I go to the store early the next morning because I want to think about something else other than the divorce. I log on to my computer, and my email notification comes alive. The district manager sent one that I missed. *Crap, did I call him back? Last he heard, Kim had just chewed me out, and I hadn't followed up with him.* I read his email:

Joel,

I haven't heard back from you about the incident in the store. I'll be by midmorning to talk to you and Kim about it.

John

At least John is coming to help. I look around the office and notice a pile of papers on Kim's desk. She still hasn't finished updating the pricing sheets for the pressure-treated lumber shipment we just received. I can't keep showing up to sticky notes and incomplete orders. I was an assistant manager for four years before I got a crack at managing my first store. This will be my opportunity to speak my mind.

I turn on the radio to the classic rock station, 98.3 KBPW-FM, as I prepare to start the workday.

"Ahh," I say with a smile and turn up the volume as I listen to a song about seeing a clear, bright future after hard times. *I should pick a song that reminds me of better days ahead and crank it up whenever it comes on. Every time I hear that song, it'll be a subtle reminder to think about how better days are ahead, and eventually I'll see clearly that my rain has gone.*

Around ten-thirty, I walk by the front door and notice the district manager's car in the parking lot.

"Hey, Kim, how long has that car been out in the parking lot?" I ask, pointing at the black sedan next to the boxwood hedge in the parking lot.

"I don't know . . . awhile?" she says, peeking around the corner from the shelves she's stocking.

"Well, heads up, I think that's the DM's car," I say, pretending to scramble in panic.

Kim quickly shuffles off to the warehouse. My other employees—Joanne, Lucas, Patricia, and Cedric—all scramble, trying to look busy.

Finally, I see John slowly walking up to the front door, taking a long look at the new glass.

"Morning, everybody! Morning, Kim," he says enthusiastically. "The doors look just like they're supposed to."

"Good morning, John," Kim replies.

"Hey, John. What's going on?" I say casually.

"Hey, just making my way through the district and stopping at a few stores, and I wanted to swing by and see how things were coming along here. Do you have a minute, Joel?" John asks.

"Yeah, sure," I say, and we head back to the office. "Can you watch the floor, Kim? We'll be just a minute."

"All right," she says, smiling.

As we make our way into the office, John sits on the computer chair across from my desk. "I wanted to come by and speak individually to the both of you about what's going on in the store," he begins. "I was looking at your profit and loss reports for the last couple of months, and you're right. Sales are 5 percent backward this month and 7.5 percent the previous month," he says, pulling out papers from his briefcase and handing them to me.

Looking at the various reports, I say, "It seems that lately Kim does not want to help. I asked her to help out with my schedule because I've worked six days a week for the last three to four weeks. She tried working six days last month and said that it was too much and she couldn't do it. She said that I get paid more, so I should work more." I laugh at the thought. "I brought up that it's likely that in the future, she will end up needing to work fifty-plus hours a week or six-day weeks, and I gave examples of scenarios currently playing out in the district."

"Did you ask her what she would do?" John asks, crossing his left leg over his right.

"I did," I respond, raising my eyebrows. "She claims that she would work those schedules then but doesn't want to do it now. I told you — stuff happens when you're not around."

We sit in silence for a moment. Then John suggests, "Maybe if we sat and talked about what was working and what areas need improvement, we could hash this out together?"

"I'm willing to try," I say. "I can use something to focus on. Angela and I are getting divorced."

"Oh no, that sucks," he says, frowning at the news. "Well, don't put too much pressure on yourself," he adds compassionately.

"Thanks, John," I say.

"Would you tell Kim to come in here?" he asks, shifting the conversation. "I'll chat for five to ten minutes with her and then will call you back in here. I want to have a debriefing wrap-up discussion. All right?"

"Sure thing." I go out to get Kim.

I go about my business, but finally I look at the clock and realize that it's been forty-five minutes. I wonder what's going on. It's 11:25

a.m. when John eventually comes out of the office. He looks tired, as though they've been talking the entire time.

"Joel, can you come in here now?" John asks.

"Yeah, no problem," I say, and walk in. I lean against the wall as John is now sitting in my chair and Kim is in the other chair, facing him.

"You know," he starts, "Kim has only been here for a few months and could benefit from more responsibility, so she knows what being a manager involves. Maybe you could let her help with some of the tasks you have versus just having her do assistant manager duties—like making the schedule for a couple of weeks. See what she thinks works for her and go from there. Maybe let her lead some of the meetings as well."

"Let her do *what?*" I say, with a bit of surprise. "Lead store meetings? You just said she's only been here for a few months. How does it make sense for her to run store meetings and make the schedule when she doesn't know what's going on? At least we could have her work for six months first. I've been working here for six years now, and I'm just getting to do those things."

I turn to Kim and say, "Kim, you are a very hard worker. You're taking information in. You're trying to train staff so they can improve performance in the store. You stress the importance of measure twice, cut once. I want you to keep working with customers and continue gaining that experience."

"You are not treating me like an assistant manager!" she exclaims, pointing her finger at me.

"What are you talking about? How am I not being fair?" I ask.

"You keep giving me these little jobs, like stocking the shelves, but not much responsibility, like I can't do anything. I told you I could help you with the scheduling. I can get people to work around the store. Look how organized the warehouse is," she says, bringing up the few areas that are organized because of her work. "My daddy gave me tips he learned when he worked in a store down south. I can do more than you're giving me credit for."

"If you could finish the orders that are given to you now, I would give you more responsibility, but your numbers aren't in the target range for more just yet," I say. I feel like this is rational thought, but John disagrees.

"Listen," he chimes in. "Delegate to Kim once in a while so she feels she's part of the management team."

Before the meeting wraps up, Kim adds, "Sometimes I don't like the way you talk to me, Joel. You treat me like I'm stupid. Like I'm not going to get anything right. John, Joel is mean to me when you're not around. He doesn't give me a fair schedule even though I ask him all the time for more help because I'm tired."

Well, it looks like I've been thrown under a bus again.

✱ ✱ ✱

Over the weekend, I go back to the house to officially move my things out and into Evan's. As the garage door opens, I feel a sense of relief because Angela's not home. I can move my stuff in peace. I park my car and go inside.

I go downstairs to the finished basement, which was supposed to be my "man cave." I see that Angela has already taken down my framed hockey jerseys that I'd hung on the wall. I shake my head.

Doing the inventory, there's the TV, my couch, and the table, which is hers. I walk into the laundry room. Here there are a few items—my old hockey equipment, storage bins of yearbooks, and photo albums. *I've got to be sure to get those out of here*, I think. *I'll take what's valuable out of here first.* Evan and Lucas will be here soon with their trucks to help me move, so I decide to get started.

I walk into the office. My books will need a box. My collection of setlists from concerts I've gone to are coming too. Wait. "What the heck?" I say, noticing something in the garbage can from the corner of my eye while I'm taking the framed souvenirs off the wall. It's my bobblehead. Not from a sporting event, but the custom bobblehead Angie had given me last Christmas. I don't know how she found this website, but they make custom bobbleheads for people. Angie had sent pictures of me and selected the action pose for my bobbling mini. It was hilarious. My bobblehead looked just like me in my adult recreation league hockey uniform, complete with my name and number on a white jersey and our alma mater's red logo on the front. The details were impressive. I thought it looked exactly like me. It was weird but so cool to have a six-inch version of me.

This bobblehead, however, has had the shit beaten out of it.

I pull the bobblehead out of the garbage can and see that its face has been smashed and its neck has been stretched as far as it could go.

"What the hell?" I say out loud.

I imagine Angie swinging it over her head angrily, stretching my little neck as far as it could go, and smashing the head against my desk here. Through tears, I yell, "I have to get out of this house!" I put my head in my hands and continue crying. At this point, why hold back?

It hits me like a ton of bricks square in the chest. This divorce is not going to be easy. Angie's pissed and hurting, but just because she's hurting and upset, that doesn't give her the right to come in here and destroy things. This is the point of no return. I'm so angry that I'm on the edge of falling apart. "Just because I'm leaving, it doesn't mean that I don't care or that I'm not hurting too," I say out loud.

After I start to calm down some, I walk into the kitchen and pull out a paper pad and a pen from our junk drawer. I take a deep breath and start to write.

Angela,

I'm sorry that you're hurting. I went to the office downstairs and saw my bobblehead destroyed. We may be getting divorced, but destroying each other's belongings is not okay. I will be sure to contact Gordon about this for documentation in the divorce proceedings.

Joel

P.S. This is not easy for me either. Please just let me go.

* * *

In the three months I've been living at Evan and Mel's, things feel like they're coming along. Thankfully they've agreed to watch Presley while I take a brief vacation to visit Andre for what remains of my relationship-recovery trip to Florida.

As I look out the plane's window, I think about my original plans for this trip. It was supposed to be an opportunity for Angela and me to bond. To go somewhere where there are beautiful things to see and do together and hang out with my old friend from high school.

But it's not a "save the marriage" trip anymore. It's a "Joel is recovering and trying to figure out what is next" trip. I have been looking forward to this trip and hope that Andre has something fun lined up to do. I need something outside of the stress of work and moving. I've been working six days a week, and Kim is still not helping out at the store.

Customer traffic is down 12 percent, and Kim has started calling HR whenever I reprimand her for being late, document her tardiness, or note tasks she is not completing.

I need this trip.

There are many smiling faces on this 727 the closer we get to landing in West Palm Beach. I haven't spent much time in Florida except for a spring break weekend in college years ago. Deep down, I do feel lonely. Something inside feels bad that I'm traveling by myself, but I'm also looking forward to seeing what happens and who I can meet. I want to hang out with Andre, have some fun, and get out of the shell I've crawled into. Maybe I will see some cool stuff, like alligators. That'd be fun.

I walk out of the airport with my carry-on and see Andre by the curb.

"Hey, brother, what's going on, man?" Andre says excitedly, as he climbs out of his SUV.

"Oh, I'm all right. How are you doing?" I say with nervous excitement.

"I'm good, brother. How was the flight?" he asks, giving me a hug.

"It was all right," I say. "I had a little extra leg space on the plane with Angie not joining me, so I got a little rest."

"Hell yeah, that's good. We're going to be up for a bit, so I'm glad you got to rest," Andre says as we get into his SUV. We're on Southern Boulevard in no time.

"So, what do you want to do?" Andre asks.

"Hey man, I'm on vacation," I say with a big grin. "I've got so much going on, and I've been working six days a week at the store for months now. I'd love to go somewhere we can chill and hang out for a little bit."

"If you want, we can head back to the house, or we can hit up a spot and have a few drinks," he says, weaving aggressively in and out of traffic.

"Do you want to grab a drink? I'm ready to start the vacation," I say.

"If you're ready, I know the perfect patio spot for us to post up. It's called Big Shots. It's near my place in Royal Palm. I've also got deep-sea fishing with Sam Braden lined up for tomorrow, so we're going to get up early."

Andre quickly changes lanes on Southern Boulevard, seemingly without looking in his mirror or signaling.

"Hey man, I'm down to be out and around people, but can you not kill us on the way there? I just got here, bro," I say, reaching for the grab handle over the window.

"Calm down, Joel. You gotta drive aggressively here. Relax, man," Andre says nonchalantly, still weaving through traffic between the red lights we keep catching.

"I just want to hang out and be in a fun environment," I say.

"I love this place," Andre says. "There are lots of TVs set up, and there's a great drink selection. You'll like it."

"I'm excited to see you, man," I say.

"Me too. It's been a minute," he responds.

We pull into the parking lot of Big Shots, and I comment, "Man, this place is nice." It's like an upscale sports bar with an outdoor tiki bar patio. The giant shot glass neon sign out front is a creative attention grabber. It looks as if it's pouring a shot.

"I told you," Andre says.

There's an outdoor lake with a water fountain just outside the patio, and there are palm trees everywhere. The covered patio has a bar and lots more seating than inside.

"Are there gators in there?" I asked, imagining one charging out of the water and toward the bar.

"I don't think so, but a rule of thumb down here is that if you see a body of water, expect alligators. If you go poking around over there, you're on your own, brother," he says with caution.

"Maybe we can see a gator somewhere else?" I suggest.

"Eh, maybe." Andre doesn't really sound too excited about it.

As we walked into the fenced-in patio bar, it's like everybody knows Andre.

"Hey, Misty," he says, hugging one of the waitresses as we walk in. "This is my buddy, Joel. He's visiting from up north."

"Hi," I say awkwardly to the attractive young blonde. She's wearing a tank top, with her tattoos proudly on display. We continue making our way to an open table, and Andre shakes hands with a few middle-aged patrons and hugs another waitress.

As we sit down, Andre asks, "So, man, what's going on? What do you want out of coming down here? What were you and Angie planning to do?"

"Well, I was hoping for us to do some sightseeing, maybe see some gators, and enjoy being in a beautiful spot," I answer. "Just explore and experience some beautiful weather in February. We don't have this up north." I'm still taking in the beauty of the outdoor space and admiring the way the bar is constructed with wood paneling and overhead fans to keep the air in circulation.

"Yeah, that's true," Andre agrees.

"I thought we would be forced to communicate more and do activities together and see what we wanted to see. We'd be doing something new and fun," I continued to explain.

"So, let me get this straight. You've been married for two years, and now you're getting divorced. How did you know Angela was the one?" Andre asks.

"You know, that's the question I've been wrestling with. I don't . . . I . . . I just . . ." I couldn't find the words to explain and began stuttering. "It . . . it seemed like it made sense. I thought we had a lot of the same interests. We both had a lot of friends, but I guess you can only party for so long," I say, realizing a lack of substance in my relationship.

"That's what you based getting married on?" he asks with surprise.

"I don't know if I asked myself," I admit. "Angie is an all-American girl with a nice family. We both have good backgrounds. It seemed like settling down in Iowa was a nice, safe thing to do. It's not like there are shootings like Chicago or LA. We're talking Des Moines here. I love Iowa because it's underrated. People only picture cornfields and, well, cornfields. No one knows what's really in the city."

On the surface I had an answer to explain my situation, but I wasn't sure where I'd actually gone wrong.

"I don't know. I'm still struggling with it," I continue.

"Well, man, I tell you what—I didn't like Angela when I met her in the first place. When I came up for the wedding, I knew right away. It seemed like you were faking it and trying to force yourself."

"Yeah? Why didn't you say anything?" I'm surprised by Andre's admission.

"It was your wedding weekend, man. Am I going to come up on the week of the wedding and tell you something's wrong with your fiancée?" he says, making his point.

"I get it, and I appreciate you telling me now. It could've been helpful, though," I say.

"Yeah, well," he says with a sigh, ending the conversation.

"Yeah," I repeat. "Why did I feel like she was such an ideal partner and the one to marry?"

I had been so confident. We got along, and our families and friends got along. "It seemed like the next logical thing to do, I guess," I say as the waitress finally comes by for our drink order.

"Well, now look at you. You're pretty fucking unhappy," Andre says, with a bit of a smirk.

"Man, did I tell you what I saw when I was moving out?" I say with new energy after I order a beer. "Angie destroyed my bobblehead. And I mean, she really must've slammed my little head on the table."

"Oh no! That little hockey deal you had sitting on your desk? Man, that thing was hilarious and looked just like you. I still gotta get me one of those," Andre says, laughing as he remembered what it used to look like.

"It's like she thinks this is easy for me," I exclaim.

"She's back there fucking up your shit. That's no good. Man, if my girl was fucking up my shit, I'd sue the shit out of her and throw her ass on the street. Ain't nobody going to be fucking up my shit," he says aggressively.

"Well, I didn't think she would be tearing my stuff up either. I've heard divorce is one of the worst experiences, and I guess it is," I say, shrugging my shoulders. "Who knows what all she's destroyed . . ."

Seemingly not paying attention, Andre interrupts. "Hey man, there's a girl over there that keeps checking you out. You should go talk to her."

I glance over to my right, noticing an intoxicated-looking twentysomething looking in my direction and flashing a smile. "Um, yeah . . . uh," I stammer again. "The divorce isn't exactly finalized until next month."

Waving his hand and dismissing my excuse, Andre says, "You aren't living with Angie anymore, and you're on vacation, man. It's not like you're in the same area code or anything. What do you owe her? Let your hair down."

"Let my hair down?" I respond. "It's not like I can turn off my emotions, man. I still have feelings for Angela." I sigh, struggling to find my words. "Deep down, I feel like I'm trying to hold it together. Like I'm trying not to fall apart and break down in front of everybody."

"Man, what's happened to you?" Andrew says, sounding frustrated with my continued emotional shares.

"I don't know. I'm hurting inside, man. I'm not saying I won't talk to anybody on this trip, but I just got here, and I'm not ready yet," I say. "Maybe we should get another drink."

"All right, whatever, bro. You do you. It's your trip," was the best he could respond.

"The weight I feel in my chest from the divorce is what hurts the most," I say.

"I'm hurt that you didn't come to me for advice when things were getting difficult with Angela. Why didn't you ask me for help?" Andre asks.

Andre wouldn't seek my help if one of his relationships was having trouble. I love him like a brother, but I surround myself with a different crowd when it comes to this.

"It comes down to lifestyle and the fact that you don't have the life I want. I need to consult with people who have similar relationships to what I was trying to have with Angela. I spoke with my parents, my brother, friends from college, all of whom are married. I won't seek advice from someone who isn't an example of the life I want to lead," I say bluntly.

"They were supporting my journey and what I thought I wanted. When I got what I thought I wanted, I realized it wasn't what I wanted after all. After that, we got professional help," I explain.

Even though Andre wasn't my role model when it came to relationships, I knew this trip was what I needed. It was a breath of fresh saltwater air.

CHAPTER 4

The Trip

Saturday morning, we wake up bright and early around six o'clock. Climbing into Andre's SUV, we head over to his friend Sam Braden's house. We pull into one of the many gated communities after a forty-five-minute drive, and Andre dials the call box. I hear a loud buzz, and the gate begins to open. Entering the neighborhood, the houses look surprisingly like an ordinary neighborhood of similarly framed houses, but in pink, aqua, and cool blue coastal colors. It's a very noticeable difference from the earth tones typical of homes back in Iowa. Weaving through the neighborhood, we turn left, then right, then left again and pull up at a cream-colored home with rusted water stains on the exterior, like many of the homes here.

As we pull up, we see that Sam is already outside and hitching the boat to his truck.

"What up, man?" Andre says to Sam, as he puts the car in park, and we get out. Sam stops turning the crank, and they do a little hand slap, then a high five and a hug. "This is my boy Joel from up north that I was telling you about," Andre says, pointing in my direction.

"Hey," I say, extending my hand, and we shake.

"What's up?" Sam asks with a head nod. "You ever been on a boat before?"

"No, but I'm excited. I hope we catch something," I say.

"I was out last week with the fiancée, and we caught a bunch of vermilion snapper and triggerfish," Sam says confidently. "Hopefully we have the same luck trolling around out there today."

"Awesome!" I instinctively respond, but I have no idea what he's talking about.

"Sam, you're always out on the water catching something," Andre adds.

He shrugs. "Well, I do what I can. What can I say? Let's head out. We need to hit the bait shop in Lake Park."

"Can we grab food and some drinks from that spot we went to last month? There was that grocery store across the street," Andre asks.

"Yeah, I want to get out before it gets too hot," Sam says as we climb into his truck, towing his nineteen-foot fishing boat and trailer. "Oh, and we need to make sure the tank is full too," he says, turning the key in the ignition. The truck rumbles to life as the dual exhaust growls angrily, and we start our adventure.

"Let me get this, man. I appreciate you taking us out today," I say, offering to pay for the gas we'll need as we park at the pump of a gas station near the bait shop.

"You sure? I mean, yeah. It's all good, man," he replies and jumps out of the truck.

Andre, who looked like he'd fallen asleep, turns around as the door closes and gives me a funny look.

"What?" I ask.

"You know how big the tank is on that boat, man?" he asks.

"Oh crap, no." I look out the window and see the fuel pump start. I get out and head into the gas station for some coffee and to find out how much fifty-eight gallons will cost me. I'm joined by Andre and Sam, and we grab a few snacks, drinks, and sunscreen for the trip and then make our way to the Harbor Park boat ramp.

Arriving at the boat launch, it's now eight thirty, with the sun still rising in the beautiful blue and orange morning sky. Sam and Andre are both wearing long-sleeved shirts, like experienced Floridians out in the sun, while I'm in a tank top, not realizing that we're going to be exposed to the sun and a cloudless sky out on the open water.

Sam's a pro and gets the boat in the water quickly, with some help from Andre. The three of us make our way out, passing other fishing boats and three of the biggest yachts I've ever seen, each at least one hundred feet long. The towering black-and-white ships are moored at what appeared to be private residences.

"Wow," I say in awe. I've never seen anything like it—a mansion with a private dock for your yacht.

"These boats ain't nothing," Andre says, waving his hands in a motion like he's seen bigger. Not a bad start to the trip. I lean back in the boat as we slowly make our way out to the open water.

"Are you ready for it?" Sam says with a smile and a tone of excitement.

"Drop the hammer and let's go," Andre says.

"Hang on!" Sam shouts as his engines rev up. We begin accelerating, and we're off!

I'm getting splashed with the warm water as we pick up speed, traveling about thirty-five to forty miles an hour on the open water, and I'm hanging on for the windy and wild ride.

"This is awesome!" I yell. Neither Andre nor Sam hears me over the sounds of the boat crashing against the waves and the engines humming along. I can feel the sun on my skin and understand the reason for the long sleeves. Still, I'm out here! Good thing we bought that sunscreen.

About eight miles off the coast, we begin the fishing pattern Sam swears by, which looks to me just like circling and throwing bait into the water. I've never been so far off the beach before and can barely see the coastline. It's the most beautiful blue ocean I've ever seen.

"Andre, take my picture. We're out here, and we're fishing!" I say, looking like a cheesy tourist.

"When you catch your first fish, you have to take a bite out of it. It's tradition," Sam says.

"What?" I ask with a look of disgust.

"The first fish you catch," Andre chimes in, "you've got to take a bite out of it and swallow it raw."

My stomach starts to turn. "I don't know about that," I say, pretending to be nauseous.

"Don't chicken out. Everybody's done it." Sam tries to reassure me.

"Oh, sure. Wise last words. We're so far out here, man, it's crazy. It looks a little deep," I jokingly say to Sam, who grew up on a boat and was not as amused.

For two and a half hours, we troll the waters, not catching anything. "Some days you win some, some days you lose some. I usually catch a ton of fish when I'm out here with the fiancée," Sam says with some disappointment.

As we make our way back to land, Sam looks at me and says, "Joel, you should move down here. That sandbar we went past is called Peanut Island, and the parties there are sick."

Andre adds, "Yeah, man. The parties are nuts. You saw those boats. Can you imagine hundreds of boats moored next to one another? The water is ankle-deep on Peanut, and everyone's walking around, drinking, and having a good time. You'd love the eye candy."

"Yeah, man." Sam continues the pitch to persuade me to move to Florida. "You don't want to stay in that Iowa snow you got up north. You could have this," he says, stretching his arms out in the sunshine. "It's 75 degrees and sunny. Do you see a cloud in the sky?"

I didn't, and he has a point, but I don't know about moving down here. "Nah, I just got my store manager position," I say, declining the offer. "Right now, my life is in such a transition, I have no idea which end is up."

"Think about it, Joel," Sam responds, raising his sunglasses and looking at me.

"Let's grab lunch back at Big Shots," Andre suggests.

"Why not? We haven't caught anything for lunch," Sam says.

"That sounds like a good idea, Andre. I'm in," I agree, giving the final vote.

When we arrive back at Big Shots, Andre starts making calls to see who wants to meet up for lunch and drinks. I order the first round of drinks at the bar with Sam. It's the middle of the afternoon and not very busy yet. There's a mix of gray hair and young souls enjoying lunch and the beautiful South Florida weather. We sit down with Andre at the same table we were at the night before, and I overhear Andre on the phone.

"Hey man, it's Dre. What are you up to tonight? I got a buddy in town who is getting divorced, and I'm trying to show him a good time. Do you wanna step out tonight?" There's a pause and Andre begins nodding his head and smiles. "That's what's up. All right, meet us at Big Shots," he says and ends the call.

"Who was that?" I ask.

"Do you remember Raymond Frost from high school?" Andre asks, continuing to scroll through his phone. "He was the kid who moved to Canada to play hockey before graduation."

"Yeah?" I say, not quite sure I actually remember him.

Andre nods his head, looking at his phone, then puts it back in his pocket. "His parents moved down from Harrisburg a few years ago, and he just moved down here not long ago," Andre explains.

"No shit? Raymond Frost is down here? It's been a long time, and it'll be good to catch up," I say. I vaguely remember that Ray was a goalie when I met him during junior year of high school. He was an up-and-coming goaltender at sixteen years old and moved to Canada with an opportunity to continue his development.

"Yeah, he said he'll be here in an hour," Andre continues, reaching for his beer and taking a sip.

"Oh," Andre says, perking up like he's been struck by lightning. He pulls out his ringing phone. "I got another buddy calling me now. Good timing," he says. "Trouble! What's going on?" he yells into the phone.

Trouble? Who's got a friend named Trouble? That can't be good. Andre starts laughing out loud. "Shit—come on, man, why are you gonna bring that up? Nah, it ain't like that. We're cool," he says with a smile. "Yeah, what are you up to? Ray called you? Yeah, my buddy Joel is down here from Iowa, and he's getting divorced, so we're out here at Big Shots grabbing some lunch with Sam."

I take a sip of my beer and keep eavesdropping.

Andre continues, "No, we didn't catch anything. I was just starting to make some calls to put a good time together. Do you want to step out tonight?" He starts laughing hysterically again. "If anybody comes out tonight, it should be you. Let me know when you drop him off and when you'll be out."

"Who was that?" I ask, curious as to who "Trouble" is and why Andre was laughing so much.

"That's my boy, Loren. We call him Trouble because sometimes he likes to run his mouth and get himself into shit. He's hilarious and knows how to party," he explains. "He lives up the road and will be here in a few. He's gotta drop his son off at his baby's mama's house first, and then he's going to make his way over," Andre says.

"All right, I guess we're going to have some fun tonight. This is a good break from the store and Angela," I say.

Trouble shows up around ten minutes later, wearing a red baseball hat backward, black jeans, and a white T-shirt with gold lettering that says Live Free or Die Young.

"Ooh, wassup," Andre says in a high-pitched voice as he stands up and greets Trouble with the traditional hug and a handshake.

"How you doing?" Trouble responds, greeting Andre.

"This is my boy Joel I was telling you about," Andre says, introducing me.

I partially stand up, extending my hand. "Joel Edmonds," I say, introducing myself formally.

"Loren Churchill," he says, shaking my hand. "They call me Trouble, or T, or whatever—man, I don't fucking care," he says, talking fast.

"You do care," Andre chimes in.

Trouble responds, "Man, people down here be talking shit so much about my nickname, man. I'm talking shit right back to you and I'm like what's up?"

I'm already getting a sense that it doesn't take much to get this guy going, but he does have energy and a big smile on his face. Who knows?

"Yeah, man, so I had to drop the little man off at Mama's house, and she was over there talking shit too," Trouble continues.

"Yeah? What's with her today?" Sam asks, joining the conversation.

"Man, she wants a couple hundred dollars a month so she can go and get her nails done. I'm like, 'Bitch, I ain't tryin' to pay for your motherfucking lifestyle,'" he says, looking in my direction.

I immediately feel a sense of relief that my divorce doesn't include a kid and have baby mama drama. I'd hate to end up pissed off like he seems to be.

"One night," Andre says, shaking his head.

"One night, and now I'm in some fucking bullshit, caught up with this motherfucking kid," Trouble complains.

"Man, you aren't caught up in shit," Sam says in a mellow tone, jumping into the conversation again. "You were dating Taryn for like two or three years before you had Baby J."

"Fucking off and on, bro," he justifies. "And she still started talking shit when she got pregnant."

"Well, damn, man," I say. "I'm going through a divorce right now up north, and she's putting me through some bullshit too."

"I'm trying to tell you, man, you gotta watch out," Trouble says, giving his two cents worth of advice.

"What's getting me," I begin, "is this 'happy wife, happy life' thing. Like, does it not matter what I want? All of a sudden, I'm married and have to just say yes to everything that she wants, and it's OK to ignore what I want? I'm like, what about me?"

"Yeah, see, man, that's what's fucked up. That's why I didn't marry Taryn," Trouble goes on.

Our waitress walks up, noticing Loren's arrival. "Can I get you something to drink?"

"Yeah, baby, you got any specials going on?"

Our waitress takes a step back and put your hands on her hips, saying, "First off, I ain't nobody's baby. You need to get your attitude together. Who do you think you are, coming in here and trying to be some sort of lame-ass Casanova?"

"Oh, shit," Sam says and starts laughing.

"That's cold-blooded, Cindy," Andre says to the waitress. Of course, he knows her too.

"Why you got to be like that?" Trouble continues.

"Because every time you come in here, you start talking shit, and I ain't nobody's baby," she continues. "Don't call me 'baby.' I just turned twenty-one."

"You're cool. Don't worry about him," Sam says, trying to calm the situation.

"Don't you have a sense of humor?" Trouble says jokingly. "We're in here all the time messing around."

"Well, I might fuck with your boy Dre, but I don't fuck with you," she said, waving a finger in his face again.

"Fine. Can you get us a round of Big Shots tequila? And I'll take a double vodka soda," Trouble says, trying to save face. She takes the order and walks over to the bartender.

I look at Andre. "You know her well?"

He shrugs it off as if they're just friends. "No, we're cool. You know me, I got friends everywhere, man," he says.

A few minutes later, Cindy comes up with Trouble's drink and four shot glasses.

"Hey, Cindy, can you bring a couple of the Big Shot Buckets for me and my boy?" Andre asks, giving a chin-up nod in my direction.

I look at the menu on our table, reading the advertisement for the bucket drink specialty they're known for here: *A bucket of southern whiskey liqueur, light rum, sweet and sour, orange and pineapple juice, topped with dark rum, garnished with an orange wheel, and cherries.*

"Oh boy, looks like we're going for it tonight," I say excitedly.

"I'll pass," Sam says. "I've still got to get the boat back home, but you all go forth and be down."

The bucket drinks arrive, and our four-person table begins to fill up with beer bottles, tequila shots, and the two yellow plastic buckets of the Big Shots signature drink.

"You can't rush drinking these," Andre says, trying to fit his mouth around the fifteen straws sticking out. I lean in and sniff. A sweet aroma catches me off guard, and my mouth begins to water.

"Wow, this smells delicious," I say before taking a drink. Taking my first sip, I say, "Mmm, this tastes like trouble."

"All right now," Trouble says, jokingly raising his eyebrows and nodding his head. "Don't end up fucked up like me with a kid after tonight. That's what got me—that damn drink," he says, shaking his finger.

"What got you was the second bucket you tried to finish," Andre chimes in.

"Get this, Joel," Trouble says, "the first time I had those, they fucked me up, and I blacked out and ended up hooking up with Taryn. I don't fuck with those anymore," he continues, shaking his head.

"And your nickname stuck," Sam says jokingly.

After my first couple of sips, I'm already starting to feel it.

Twenty minutes later, Ray shows up, looking ten years older than I remembered him. He reminds me of a mature young adult hanging on to his youth. It's about five o'clock now, and the bar is picking up.

"Hey, Joel," Trouble says, "let's go talk to those girls over there at the bar." My liquid courage is kicking in, and I turn around, remembering the girl Andre pointed out earlier. I am up for conversation now, but I notice she has already left and a new group has taken her place.

"Do you want to go see what's up?" I ask Trouble. I haven't cold-approached a girl I was attracted to since I met Angela four years ago.

"Come on," Trouble says, standing up from our table. "Be my wingman."

"What's the harm in going to say hi?" I reply, shrugging my shoulders. "I'm in."

We make our way over to talk to a blonde and a brunette sitting in the corner, and I notice that my legs aren't entirely stable under me. The bucket has affected me more than I realized, and I try to shrug it off.

"Hey, ladies, what's going on?" Trouble says, followed by silence. "My name is Loren, and this is my buddy Joel, visiting from Des Moines, Iowa. I was just telling him about the beautiful people down here and couldn't help but notice you two sitting over here. Are you enjoying your evening?"

"Yeah, I'm Sandra, and this is Diane," says our new blonde friend. Diane gives us a half-smile.

"I'm Joel," I say to Diane.

"Hi," she says, with a clear lack of interest.

"Sorry, I'm kind of nervous," I continue. "I apologize for the tank top. I was on a boat earlier today."

"Oh, yeah?" Another short reply and silence. She begins to stir her drink.

"Whatever, bro," Trouble cuts in. "It's Florida, and it's hot. It's totally fine to wear a tank top. Anyway, we just wanted to see if you want to hang out. We wanted to invite the two of you to join our table."

He continues, "See, our crew is over there," pointing toward our table. "That's my boy Andre over there—he's hosting and lives around the corner, and that's Raymond."

"We're good," Sandra says coolly. "We're just enjoying our drinks and are going to head out soon. But thanks for coming over."

"Well, if you change your minds and want to hang out, it'd be good to get to know you ladies."

"Well, thanks, Loren," Diane says. Smiling at me, she says, "Maybe we'll change our minds." I start sweating; I've barely had my ring off my finger and now here I am, standing in Florida talking to women at a bar.

I say to Diane, "Andre is putting together a good time tonight for us. I get that I look like a scrub, but we went fishing earlier and haven't been home yet. I do clean up pretty well. We'll change before heading out. Maybe I can give you a call then?"

"Hmm, maybe," she responds. "Give us a minute."

"Right on," I say. "Enjoy the rest of your evening if I don't get to say goodbye." I turn to walk back to the table; Trouble has already left.

Andre is so excited. "Oh man, you guys looked like you were struggling! Shot down!" he says, laughing. "Joel, you still got no game."

"No game?" I reply. "I was talking to someone new."

I look at Raymond. "You can't go forward if you don't at least try and start somewhere," I say.

"Nah, man, that's some bullshit," Andre says. "Finish up your drinks. We're heading to the strip club in a little bit."

"Strip club? Why would we go to a strip club when we're already at a bar? I told Sandra and Diane that we'd be here for a bit. Let's get one more round and hang out for a while," I suggest, still hopeful.

The girls never came over.

We start barhopping, trying to find a place to hang out. Andre seems to only want to go to dive bars. "You guys sure you don't want to go to a strip club?" he suggests again, and with all the dead ends, the rest of the crew doesn't seem to care anymore. I'm just along for the ride now.

We start at the first gentleman's club, and sit at the bar. Raymond is drunk, and Trouble looks more intoxicated than Andre or me. It gets old quickly, and I'm fending off requests to spend money in the Champagne Room. Andre, spotting an open table near the front of the stage, motions to a server to seat us there.

"Yo, let's get a table up front," Andre says with excitement.

"You look tense. Do you want a shoulder massage?" I hear as soon as I sit down. A young woman, wearing little and leaving nothing much to the imagination, is carrying a basket of lotions.

"Sure," I say, relenting to the constant pressure of services and experiences offered.

"Twenty-five dollars," she says.

Silly me for using a fifty-dollar bill Andre had given me earlier to cover part of the gas as a payment for a twenty-five dollar back massage that lasts about two and a half minutes.

"All right, thanks," she says, tapping me on the back.

"Um, can I get change for that fifty I handed you?" I ask.

"We don't give change," she says, giving me a funny look.

"Well, then I've got twenty-five bucks' worth left," I say. She gives me an unenthusiastic shoulder rub for two more minutes. *This place is a freaking rip-off. I should know better.*

I turn to Andre, who is sitting to my left. "Twenty-five bucks for two and a half minutes? What is that?" I ask.

"You should've known better, bro," he says, keeping his eyes fixed on the dancer onstage.

I look confused and say, "How am I going to know that? Why would I even want to know that?"

"Hey, man, you're the one who spent fifty bucks on a back massage," Raymond jokes through slurred speech.

"A mediocre shoulder massage at best. Lesson learned! I'm keeping my wallet in my pocket," I declare.

Andre motions to our waitress to come over to the table and whispers something in her ear. She smiles and walks off.

"I got us bottle service. If we don't finish it, we can come back and get it later," he says with excitement.

"Come back and get it? Who comes back to get a bottle of alcohol from a strip club?" I start wondering what I got myself into on this trip.

"Hey, Trouble, do you want to head out?" I ask.

"What do you mean, head out?" Andre jumps in. "I just ordered a bottle."

"I'm not feeling it being here. I'm dealing with the divorce, and the last place I want to be is at a loud strip club," I say as a new dancer takes the stage.

"Come on, man, you gotta give it a chance. You're not used to having a good time," he says, turning his attention back to the exotic moves on stage.

"If this is having a good time, I'm cool with chilling back at the house and relaxing for a little bit. Trouble was saying earlier he was feeling tired, and I can jump a ride with him," I suggest.

"Man, don't get in the car with him. I am telling you." Andre looks at me with a serious look. "You're making a stupid decision getting out of here with him."

"Hey, I'm just not feeling like hanging out here. If we went to a sports bar or dance club, maybe I'd be up for it. Tell your fiancée I'm on my way back, and I'll catch a rideshare."

"No, man, I'm not going to have you come down here and then call for a rideshare. We came together, we'll leave together," he insists.

"I'm not trying to make us all leave," I say, not wanting to ruin the mood for everyone.

"You're over here pouting in the corner," Raymond says.

"I told you, I'm getting divorced, man. It's not like I'm here celebrating. I'm not exactly excited about it," I say.

"You need to lighten up and let that stupid-ass bitch go. I never liked her anyway," Andre says.

"Whoa, man. You're crossing the line," I say, leaning back in my chair.

Trouble also jumps in. "Yeah, man. It's not like you ain't dated no stupid-ass bitches. What are you judging him for? Leave that man alone and look at your own shit." Andre flips out and shoves Trouble over the couch of the VIP booth we're in.

"Over what he said to you?" I scream over the music. "What the hell is wrong with you?" I help Trouble get on his feet.

"That's what he does," Andre screams.

"What do I do? Call you on your shit when you're trying to put somebody down?" Trouble spikes back.

"You jump into conversations, and you start talking shit," he yells. As expected, security comes running toward the booth with the commotion and yelling.

I lose my cool and shove Andre, yelling, "Whoa! You need to calm down! You just crossed a line!" Bouncers surround me and angrily make a way toward the exit. Everyone is in an uproar.

Andre knows the bouncers here, too, and calls out, "Of course, this asshole is visiting me from Iowa. He doesn't know any better."

Following us toward the door, he says to one of them, "My bad, Jason. You know I'm here to have a good time."

Once we're outside and security has turned me loose, Andre asks, "Dude, what's the problem?"

"Are you kidding me? You're asking me what the problem is right now? Did you not hear what you just said?" I yell at him.

Again, he asks, "Seriously, what's your problem, man?"

"Did you not hear what you just said?" I repeat. "Now you're asking me what *my* problem is and why *I'm* upset?"

He unlocks the doors to his SUV, and we head back to his place to call it a night.

"I appreciate that you warned me not to get in the car with Trouble. I just wanted to chill. At least we didn't get arrested," I say, breaking the silence.

This trip is not turning out to be the fun, relaxing experience I was hoping for.

CHAPTER 5

Help Wanted

"Knock, knock," I hear through the door outside my bedroom.
"Ugh," I groan.
"Joel, are you alive?" It's Andre's fiancée, Monica.

Ugh, yeah. Barely. Hold on, let me open the door," I say and slowly roll myself out of bed. "Oh, boy." My first steps feel like a newborn baby deer trying to figure out how to stand up, and I stumble, falling back on the bed.

"You OK?" I hear through the door.

"Yeah, I'm coming," I say. My head is throbbing, and I groan even louder as I open the door.

"Hey, how are you doing?" she says, chuckling at my disheveled nature, wearing last night's clothes.

"I feel like I've been hit by a truck," I say in a dry, raspy voice.

"I bet. You look like it. I brought you some water and something for your headache," she says, handing me a glass and two tablets.

"Thanks." I take the pills and drink all the water. "That Big Shots Bucket kicked my ass."

"Oh no, Dre got you one of those? How many did you have?" Monica asks.

"One. He was buying shots too. Ugh, I don't even remember how many beers we drank," I say, rubbing my forehead.

"Wow, you guys must have been going hard last night. What time did you get back? I heard a commotion, but it was pretty late."

"I don't know what time it was, but it was late. What time is it now?" I ask.

"It's going on eleven," she says, looking at the clock on her smartwatch.

"Eleven?" I repeat and groan again. I head for the kitchen to get more water.

"Did you have a good time? Andre likes those buckets," Monica asks.

"Did Andre tell you what happened last night?" I ask, dodging the question.

"No, he's still asleep. I figured I'd check on you in case you don't typically sleep in like he does."

"Thanks. Last night was no good. I told him at one point that I wanted to come home and chill, and he lost his shit and started talking about Angela, and it set me off," I explain.

"Oh no. I'm so sorry," she says, covering her mouth. "What did he say?"

"He called her some names I won't mention, and then he and his friend Trouble got into an argument that turned into a shoving match in the middle of a strip club, and we got kicked out. I'm not sweating Andre's drama," I say.

"You guys went to The Blue Flower last night?" she asked with surprise. Monica was quiet for a moment, looking like she's stewing about something.

"I'm sorry," she says again, breaking her silence, and sits down on the chair adjacent to the loveseat I've curled up on.

I reach out for the glass of water I've poured for myself and take another big drink, groaning again.

"What time is your flight?" she asks.

"Um, around five, but I honestly don't even want to be around Andre right now. I think I want to go to the airport. I might jump in the shower and call a rideshare."

"You're gonna leave? I thought we were going to brunch today. Andre has been talking about taking you to his favorite brunch spot in downtown West Palm," she says, disappointed with the news.

"Well, I don't know about that," I say, rocking myself forward to stand up.

"So, what are you going to do? Hang out at the airport?" she asks with a confused look.

"Yeah, I guess," I say with a yawn and a big stretch.

"What happened last night that was so bad?" she asks, trying to understand my sudden departure.

"Andre crossed the line. I wanted to come down here and be around friends having a good time. Andre is usually so upbeat and supportive," I say.

"Well, you know his heart's in the right place, and he means well," Monica says in Andre's defense.

"Maybe. I'm going to shower," I say and get up. "I really appreciate you letting me stay here, Monica."

"Of course. We love hosting," she says, heading toward the kitchen. "I don't know what's going on with Andre. He was excited that you were coming," she adds with a frown.

Getting out of the shower, I can hear Andre in the hallway having a heated conversation with Monica about me leaving early.

"Fuck him. I don't want to deal with his sensitive ass either. Who does he think he is?" I hear. I finish changing, and as I begin to make my way back to the bedroom to get my stuff, I pass Andre in the hall.

"Hey bro, I'm sorry about last night. I didn't mean to . . ."

He stops and pauses. "You're just too sensitive sometimes when I'm real with you about what's going on."

He doesn't even make it through an apology.

"Well, thanks, but no thanks. I don't need your criticism, and I don't want to hear your opinion about Angela. I'm not happy with you," I say. "Especially since I traveled a thousand miles down here from Des Moines. I've been getting my ass kicked at work, and I'm dealing with the divorce. Whatever, man. You do you."

"I'm not the one worried about it. You're the one who got so upset. And Monica said you're not coming to brunch now?" Andre says, shifting his tone.

"No. I need some space, and I'm going to call a ride to the airport," I say.

"When's your flight?" Andre asks. "I thought it was later."

"It's in a few hours—don't worry about it," I say, waving him off.

"Well, let me at least drive you to the airport," he offers.

"I appreciate the offer, but I'm going to pass."

"Are you serious?" he says.

"Yeah, I'm serious," I say. "Right now, I've got some stuff I need to figure out, and last night was an eye-opener for me. I'll let you know when I get back to Des Moines. Thank you for letting me stay here and showing me around."

"Whatever, man," Andre says and storms into his bedroom, slamming the door behind him.

I turn to look at Monica and shrug my shoulders. Then I call for my ride to the airport.

****

Back home, I've scheduled myself to work a few hours on Monday, midday, to catch up on pressing issues, if any, and I plan to leave early to meet Bart Honer and watch the Iowa Grizzlies play Rockford.

Walking into the office from the back door, I notice a stack of papers piled on Kim's desk that she obviously hasn't filed yet. I look at the clock on the wall, and it's eleven fifteen. "It's like a tornado hit in here. I've been gone for three days, and my clean office is a disaster!" I say.

I sit at my desk, which is covered with an assortment of green, orange, and blue sticky notes, crumpled papers, loose receipts, and mail. I try to make sense of it all as I log in to the computer to check our sales results and inventory levels. "Kim didn't even order inventory?" I shout. I head to the sales floor to find her and ask her how she missed ordering inventory while I was out.

"Hey, Patricia, where's Kim?" I say as I walk through the warehouse doors to the interior painting aisle.

"Hey, Joel. How was Florida?" she says with positive energy.

"It was OK. Beautiful, but not quite what I was expecting. Have you seen Kim?" I ask.

"She's gone on break, I think. She'll be back in an hour or two," Patricia insinuates.

An hour or two? "When did she leave?" I ask with a furrowed brow.

"Um, like eleven or so, I think."

"OK. I'll be in the office. I noticed that something may have been missed, and I want to get this done before it's too late," I say with frustration.

"OK," she says with a grin.

The most important thing we need to do to keep this business functioning is to ensure we have products in the store for our customers. George Martin has that job coming up in a week. At least I have some time to figure how to place an emergency order and get the material here ASAP. I take a deep breath and sigh.

As I make my way back to the office, I look at the clock on my phone and notice a customer walking in.

"Good morning, Bart," I say. "Are we still on for the game tonight?"

"You know it," he replies. "How was the trip?"

"It was OK. I didn't get to go to a hockey game, but I did go a few miles out on the ocean and met some interesting people," I say.

"That's cool," Patricia chimes in.

Just then, Lucas comes up. "Hey, man, can we talk?" he asks.

"Sure, what's up?" I say, happy to see him after my long weekend.

"I wanted to tell you about something that happened in the store while you were gone," he begins, fidgeting and looking uncomfortable.

"OK. Bart, I'll have to catch up with you at the game tonight," I say and excuse myself. "Let's head to the office to chat," I say to Lucas, leading him to the back of the store.

"OK. What's up, Lucas?" I ask as we enter the office.

"While you were out, Kim was talking to Cedric, Patricia, and Joanne about how unfairly she's being treated. I don't know what's going on, and I don't want to be involved in it," he begins.

"Are you serious?" I ask. I feel a familiar kind of stress wash over me.

"Oh yeah, man. I was walking in to start my shift on Friday, and she was yelling and waving her arms around. I'm not dealing with this attitude and back talk," he says.

"I hear you, man." At that moment, I had no idea what to say. *What do I do?*

"You don't understand, Joel. I want to progress my career with H&H and potentially be a manager, like you. That's why I came here, but I'm not dealing with this toxic attitude," he continues.

"What do you need from me, Lucas? How can I help?" I ask.

"I don't know, man. Just thought I'd let you know and leave it at that," he responds.

"I'll talk to her," I say. "You worked hard to get here, and you've done everything I've ever asked you to do."

"Thanks, Joel," he says, then leaves the office.

Sometime later, as I'm placing an emergency inventory order, my longest-tenured employee, Joanne, walks in to clock in and begin her closing shift.

"Hey, Joanne, can I ask you something?" I say.

"Sure? What's up?" She is all of four foot ten, and today her long gray hair is braided, not typical for her.

"First off, I like the hair. What did I miss?" I ask, looking at her.

"You like it? Yeah, Kim came over last night for dinner, and she asked to braid it. I didn't think she could braid my fine hair, but it's stayed so far," she says proudly.

"Wow, nice," I say. "Maybe you could help me understand something. Is Kim telling everyone she's being mistreated or something? I'd hate for her to be trying to get people to draw sides here. She's the assistant manager and she might be confused about what her role is. Do you know anything about what she said?"

"Excuse me?" Joanne snaps.

"What? I wish you could see what I see in you—in all the team here," I say. "The commitment, honesty, and integrity are incredible. You've been in this store almost ten years. I feel like we're at a point where peace is becoming difficult to find here," I explain.

"We're supposed to have one another's back when customers turn on us. We don't turn on one another," she retorts.

"What are you talking about?" I ask, very confused.

"You said I was choosing sides and that she needed to stay in her place! That poor child is working so hard on her own. You're so mean to her!" she exclaimed.

"What? Joanne, if we can't work through this together, I've failed you as the store manager. The company is looking at my name on the P&L, and right now, our sales are going backward. I'm trying to understand the store's performance," I tried to explain. "Why are you so upset?"

"Don't bring me into your mess. Talk to Kim yourself. You know she knows what she's doing. Kim's uncle is a manager in Omaha," she says, shaking her head and walking off.

Kevin, my primary supporting sales rep, walks in as Joanne is storming out. "Are you OK, kid? I've seen *that* march out of the office before." Kevin is a good mentor behind the scenes and often gives me tips he learned when he managed this store. I appreciate his timing today.

"I'm at a breaking point. I'm just getting back from my trip to Florida and there's drama spreading throughout the staff," I begin. "How did you manage this store? I need some help. Look at this office!" I say, pointing at the mess.

"Ah, kid, you know, I had to get my lumps in the store too. It's a beast, no doubt. We all have to figure out what we can do to make things work here," Kevin says.

"What worked for you?" I ask, hoping for an answer. Kevin has been successful growing his territory since he left the store. All of the relationships he developed in the store followed him when he became a sales rep.

"For me," he begins, leaning back and touching his chin, "it started with prioritization. I had to figure out the P&L and how to get Joanne to put freight away. It looks good pointing at the scoreboard now, but that's the result of many failures and easy wins to start."

"So, for me to be successful in the store, I have to find new business to replace what Kim has driven to shop elsewhere," I said, thinking out loud. "I also have to find a way to improve our relationship."

"Well, the good news is that some customers will return once Kim's out of here," Kevin begins. "But until then, you have to be the driving factor in getting this team to turn over every stone and generate new business opportunities." It was a hard truth, but he was right.

I start rubbing my head.

"How was Florida? You find someone new?" he says jokingly.

"New?" I say, confused.

"Yeah, there are girls in Florida," he says a bit sarcastically.

"That vacation I took wasn't much of a break. And Lucas told me twenty minutes ago that Kim complained to Joanne, Cedric, and Patricia about her pay, her hours, and her unfair treatment here. I just asked Joanne about it, and she said she didn't want to get pulled into my mess. That was right before you walked in."

"Employee satisfaction is essential. You need to stay informed, and if there is any disharmony with the staff, that needs to be addressed, Joel," Kevin stays sternly.

"Yeah, well, I'm finishing up an emergency inventory order now, so just add that to my list of people upset with me right now," I say, picking on myself.

"Kim didn't put that order in? I was here on Friday, and she said she was going to take care of it."

"Yeah, well, you know how that goes. She was going to throw this garbage away, too," I say, trying to be funny.

"Can I give you some words of wisdom, kid?" Kevin asks.

"Sure."

"It might serve you to look at your experience from a different perspective. Where you're at right now, you're going to burn yourself out, and you're going to make yourself miserable. I can already feel it," he says, taking a step back as though something coming from me is repelling him.

"What else am I supposed to do? I don't know how to manage a multimillion-dollar store or lead a team of people," I say, admitting my inexperience.

"I remember being in that position myself." Kevin's phone begins ringing. "Hold on. Hello?" He walks out of the office.

A minute later he walks back in, still talking. "All right, well, let me wrap up here and I'll head over."

"Who was that?" I asked.

"George Martin. He's pissed. Kim forgot to deliver something for him, and now I've got to run to the West Des Moines store to grab some gallons of fibered aluminum roof coating Kim never picked up. Do you know anything about this?" he asks, confused.

"No clue," I say, and shrug my shoulders.

"Sorry, kid, I gotta run."

"It's all good," I say, feeling discouraged.

"Check out the difference between good stress and bad stress some time—which is which, and why. Remember, what doesn't kill you makes you stronger," he says as he leaves.

"Are you sure?" I yell back.

The ability to think clearly and rationally in a stressful situation is imperative. Maybe I do need to figure out what stresses me out.

I go back to placing my order for inventory.

CHAPTER 6

Defining Purpose

I love attending hockey games at Goods Bank Arena. They have an indoor open-air vestibule for their box office, leading to a staircase with sets of stairs that lead to the ticket scanners. It's like ascending to smiling faces, excited to welcome you to the night's event. I see Bart at the top of the stairs as I walk in.

I make my way through lines of excited hockey fans buying last-minute tickets, couples out on date nights, and parents trying to figure out how to manage small children in large crowds. I succumb to the slow pace, waving to Bart, who sees me stuck in traffic.

"Good evening, sir," I say, handing my ticket to the gray-haired man at the top of the stairs. He's well dressed in a red vest, pressed white shirt, and black slacks.

"Hey, how are ya?" he responds, quickly scanning my ticket. "Enjoy the game."

"Thank you," I say and enter with a smile.

I head to my left, past the 50/50 lottery table.

"Hey, Bart," I say excitedly and extend my hand.

"Hi, Joel. How are you? How was the drive?" he says with a big smile, shaking my hand.

"I'm good. It wasn't so bad," I say, taking a look around. "It's crowded tonight. How are you?"

"I'm good. Busy, but I wanted to catch the Rockford game with you. You've asked me a couple of times to go to a game, and you're right, this looks like a must-see. I didn't know they had so many players ready to move up to Chicago in the lineup."

"Yeah, Rockford has some top prospects, and we're on the bubble to make the playoffs for the first time. Tonight will be a good game. Do you want to grab some food and a drink, then head to our seats?" I ask.

"Yeah, that sounds good. Thanks for inviting me. This is exciting," Bart says.

"No problem, Bart. You've been a good customer, and I appreciate our conversations at the counter when you come in." We head to the concession stand outside section 105.

"Where are our seats? This is my first game," Bart asks, looking around, grinning from ear to ear.

"Third row, this section," I reply. "Tonight is game twenty-six for me this season. I love it!"

"Really?"

"Yeah. Our seats are right in the corner where the big hits happen. You never know if there's going to be a fight right in front of you or something. I caught a puck one game," I say.

"Oh, man!" Bart says, getting more excited.

We grab some pizza and beer and head over to a stand-up table near the mezzanine windows overlooking the Des Moines River.

"So, Joel, how are things?" Bart asks as we begin eating. "You looked pretty stressed in the store."

"Yeah, I've got a few things going on. I'm going through a divorce, which will be finalized next month, and the store is a challenge on its own. Managing this many people and getting divorced . . . it's a lot going on at once," I say.

"It sounds tough. How are you handling it all?"

"I'm trying to do well and go above and beyond. Some employees don't want to work, and sometimes I don't know what to do. I'm starting to listen to podcasts, and some guests reference books they've written or research studies that might help me to motivate them," I explain.

"What do *you* want?" he asks, then takes a long swig of his beer.

"That seems to be a popular topic of conversation lately," I say, starting to squirm.

"No. It sounds like you're trying to figure something out," Bart says curiously.

"Well," I say, "now that I'm in a leadership position at work, people look at me like, 'I need your help. Show me what to do.' And I was in this 'happy wife, happy life' mentality that felt like I was doing what everyone else was around me. Like fall in line, and everything I'm supposed to do is planned. I feel like what I want doesn't matter anymore."

Bart nods. "Uh-huh. It sounds like you're stuck or something."

"I do feel stuck," I say. "I just got promoted six months ago, and now with the divorce, I don't know what to do to get back on my feet again."

"You know, Joel, I'm in a networking group that meets Wednesday mornings for coffee, and there's a guy who's a life coach. I'd love to introduce you to him if you're OK with me making the introduction."

"Sure? What does a life coach do? I'm not sure how he could help," I say.

"Well, from what I recall during our meetings, he helps people in transition and supports them to get unstuck in areas where they're looking to progress, creating new possibilities in their lives. Whether it's a job change, a divorce, or working on a project, he has a way of revealing what's getting in their way and blocking progress," Bart explains. "I know it's short notice, but would you be available Wednesday morning?"

"I'm just getting back from vacation, so this week might not work for me. What about next week? Or maybe I can switch shifts with Kim," I say, thinking out loud.

"Let me know. I can bring a guest once a quarter, and I'd love to introduce you to Coach Thomas. He's been coaching for about a decade now," Bart says.

"I'm only telling you this because you're one of the few I trust that come in the store. What type of stuff does he talk about?" I ask, my curiosity piqued.

"I haven't gotten coaching myself, but from his introduction, he talks about business leadership coaching and how he works with people who feel stuck and can't find a way from where they are to where they want to be."

"Bart, I appreciate this. I needed a conversation like this. My trip to Florida was pretty shitty, and my friend, whom I thought would be helpful to connect with, ended up being one of the most toxic people I've ever been around. I'll tell you about it after the national anthem. Let's head in," I say.

Bart looks like a kid in wonderland as we walk to our seats.

"Wow, Joel, this is incredible," Bart says as the public announcer comes on over the music.

"Ladies and gentlemen, welcome to Goods Bank Arena. Tonight, squaring off are the visiting Rockford Icemen and your Iowa Grizzlies!" The crowd goes moderately wild for a Monday night.

The stands are sparsely packed, and the local cable access TV cameras are rolling. As they announce the starting lineup, the players skate out of a giant inflatable grizzly bear head onto the ice across from our seats. I can tell Bart has bought into the schtick. The national anthem begins, sung by a group of middle school kids singing the words they remember. Fans in the crowd sing along to fill in the blanks, including Bart and me.

As soon as the puck drops, it's a different story. Emotion runs high.

Iowa wins the opening face-off, and the puck zips from right to left between the defensemen. The loud cracking sound of the puck hitting the stick blade is quick and precise. Iowa star Seth Jeffers cuts to the middle and receives a pass from his defenseman and is on a breakaway. Racing in our direction with the roar of the crowd cheering him on, he dekes to the left. The Rockford goalie overcommits and slides out of position but turns to swing his stick at the puck, and the puck crosses the line, bouncing over the goalie's stick, and Jeffers scores! The celebration erupts from the stands, and the Grizzlies' goal horn begins to fill the arena with high-decibel energy.

Bart and I jump out of our seats and throw our hands in the air, screaming, "Yeah!"

"Holy cow! Did you see that, Joel?" Bart looks amazed, and we high-five.

"That was so cool! They almost got it. What a shot!" I say with excitement.

The energy and "Let's go, Grizzlies!" chants ring out in unison.

Halfway through the second period, the score is 5–1, and we're getting our asses kicked.

As the puck heads down to the Grizzlies' defensive zone, I notice one of our players, Curtis Franssen, yelling at a Rockford player and drifting toward our corner. "Oh shit, Bart, heads up! Somethings going to happen," I instinctively shout out.

Just as Bart turns his head to see what's happening, both players drop their gloves and start throwing punches at each other.

Bart's eyes go wide in amazement. "I have no idea how these guys are standing there taking punches to the face and still swinging. I'd probably be on the ground for sure by now!" Bart jokes as the referees break up the fight.

"Two guys, toe to toe, swinging with everything they've got! That's intense," I respond.

"I've never seen an actual fight in person before, but that Curtis Franssen sure took a shot to the chin. Oh, boy!" Bart says, still in shock.

A few minutes after the fight, Bart leans over with a disappointed look.

"What's up?" I ask.

"I need to get going before the third period begins," he says. "I had a lot of fun, Joel. Thanks again for inviting me."

"Yeah, me too. That stinks, but it's probably not necessary to witness the end of this thumping," I say.

"Seeing the different prospects coming up is amazing from these seats! That Seth Jeffers is really good," Bart says with a big smile.

"Yeah, he can hang with the pace and belongs in the show," I remark. "He's only nineteen years old, six foot four, and about two hundred pounds. He's young, but he's a big kid."

"I'm glad I was here to see that goal. You were right about the fight being a lot different from down here," Bart says nodding his head.

"It's cool seeing the nuanced differences in everyone's game and how hard they're working out there. I love it. Making it to the next level is hard, and not everyone at this level will make the next step," I explain. "I've also been thinking about it and will ask Kim or Lucas to switch shifts to open Wednesday so I can meet this coach."

"Oh, that's good news," Bart says. The horn blows to signal the end of the second period. "I'll text you the address. The meeting starts at nine and I'm usually there by eight fifteen."

"I'll be there. Thanks again for coming tonight," I say with a big smile.

"It's been my pleasure. Thanks for having me." As he stands up to make his way past me, he sticks out his hand, and I shake it.

On the car ride home, I turn on the radio to distract myself from the Grizzlies' loss and hear lyrics being sung so compassionately:

Take my heart, hold it tight.
I can't trust the rest of my life.
Is it too soon? Should I give it time?
Will you be by my side?
Will you be my wife?

It's the hard question.
Will I keep loving?

It's so hard to stay open.
When there's heartache in my life.

I don't want to hide from you,
but love is something I'm afraid to do.
So, I ask the hard question.
And keep on loving.

The words hit me to the core, and I start to tear up. In my car, I start yelling, "This isn't fair!" I take a deep breath, yelling, "Ahh!" over and over again. Eventually I do feel better.

When I get home after the game, Evan and Mel are still out. Presley, however, is here and excited to see me.

"Hey, puppy," I say, scratching behind her ears as her tail wags and she runs around my legs. I kneel, hugging her in mid-happy dance. Walking into the guest bedroom I've been calling home, I set down my keys, grab a pen and my journal from my backpack, and begin to write:

> *Am I asking too much? Will I be OK? I want to meet this*
> *coach Bart was telling me about tonight. It's not just about my*

heart being broken. What about the anger I feel inside for being in this situation? Being told that what I want doesn't matter. I'm not accepting that. The weight and the pain and the fact that every time I hear that song, I want to cry because I resonate so well with that experience. This hurts.

***

On Tuesday, looking for a new apartment is my priority, and I apply to three apartments online before the store opens. At nine-thirty, I get a call that there's one in West Des Moines I can move into today. Once Lucas and Kim arrive for their shifts, I take a half day to arrange movers and quickly move into my new space from Evan and Mel's temporary recovery house.

As I drift off to sleep that night, I dream that I'm in Hank and Harry's, and for whatever reason, half of the lights are off while people are shopping in the store. I can't see much. It looks like the store is closing. I walk out to the parking lot and feel Angela's presence. Just then, I see her coming out of the pet store with Presley on a leash. Cars start pulling out of the parking lot stalls, and she notices me and immediately walks in my direction. The look she is giving me is terrifying as she marches toward me. I can't run.

"This 180 that you're doing—what are you not telling me? Like really, who are you?" she asks. "I see how you act now that we're married."

Wait, what? Married? I look at my left hand and notice my wedding band is back on my ring finger.

"Wait a second," I stutter, realizing that I'm still married to her. "I'm not going to be stuck with you!"

"What kind of responsibility is that?" Angela yells at me.

"There has to be another way. I feel shitty," I confess.

"That's an excuse, Joel," Angela says adamantly.

"I know! That's part of the problem. Our relationship involves too much alcohol and having a good time rather than establishing a foundation to be a couple. I don't want to be responsible for your drinking," I admit.

"You fall asleep in public, not me. I'm waking you up because you drank so much!" she yells.

"So, this is when I find out who you really are—by being married to you?" I ask.

"Yes, and you're like 'now I'm stuck with you' because you don't like me or something! We're married, Joel!" Angela shouts.

"There's always a way out," I yell in a moment of honesty.

"That's quite a sign of your commitment to leave," she says, calming down from the anger she initially approached with. "I'm not going to spend the rest of my life uncertain whether my partner loves me or not."

"I'm unsure when you're going to flip shit and do something that no one expects, like when you slapped Evan and accused Mel and me of having an affair. They're one of my most important friendships and foundational to my support network," I say adamantly, throwing up my hands.

"Why did you decide to get married in the first place? Why are you sure about the divorce now?" she asks, getting to the real reason she came over to confront me. Presley sits on the ground next to her, and cars are still entering and exiting the parking lot. I'm looking around, and no one seems to notice us.

"When I got laid off from my job after college, I had nowhere to go and wanted to move back to Iowa. Evan and Mel took me in and let me sleep on their couch for a month," I say in self-defense.

"So? This is so embarrassing," Angela says, her voice cracking. "You're making my life a miserable experience! I married you," she yells and begins crying. Presley jumps up and starts barking and panting heavily.

I sense my bottom lip starting to quiver. "You know, Evan and Mel were two of only a few people I knew in the area before I got to Hank and Harry's. They still believe in me."

"I didn't know you then," she says through tears.

"You called the fucking cops on Evan at his house that night after we put you to bed because you had too much to drink," I yell.

"I was worried," Angela says in shame.

"Are you serious?" I say in disbelief. "You pass out after drinking too much, accuse my best friend's wife of having an affair with me, and when we have a nightcap to clear the air, you call the police claiming we're plotting against you. We were literally down the street at the bar. How is this behavior OK in a marriage? You slapped my best friend," I continue.

Angela begins crying and falls to her knees. Presley is panting even more now and begins to throw up on my feet, startling me, and I wake up.

Whew, it was a vivid dream again.

Presley is panting near the bed, and it takes me a second in the darkness to figure out what's going on.

"Do you need to go outside?" I say to her. Still panting, she looks at me like she's got a big smile on her face. "OK, I'll get out of bed. We'll go out," I say, getting out of bed.

As we walk to the back door of the apartment, I think that she's strangely eager to go out at two o'clock in the morning. I prop open the door, and Presley prances out to her spot in the yard to do her business and then runs back inside.

"All better?" I say as I take off her harness. Looking at her, I see that she's still panting. I notice she is still shaking a little. "Maybe you have to go number two?" I ask.

She shivers at the sound of my voice. "Uh, oh, come on, puppy," I yell, and we run toward the back door. I open the door for her to sprint out. It's good she runs where no one can see what's about to go down.

When she's done, she trots back to the door.

"Whew, pup! That was gross!" I say in disgust.

Presley looks up at me, wagging her tail as though she appreciates the relief. As we walk down the hall again, she veers off to the bathroom and throws up on the floor.

"Of course," I say. *The poor dog was holding it in from both ends.* Presley sits in the bathroom doorway, looking like she finally feels back to normal. "Like nothing happened," I say, grabbing the bathroom cleaning supplies from under the sink and starting to clean up the laminate wood flooring.

***

That Wednesday, I arrive at The Midtown on Grand at 8:40 a.m. The formal part of the morning networking meeting begins in twenty minutes. I park my car and walk in.

The conference room is packed with twenty to thirty people, all already in conversation and wearing name tags.

"Hey, Joel," I hear from behind me.

I turn around and it's Bart, with his big smile. His curly hair is noticeably styled as opposed to the typical baseball cap he usually wears.

"Good morning, Bart. Sorry I'm running behind. My dog got sick last night, and I was up with her in the middle of the night," I say.

"Oh wow. How's your dog now?" he asks with concern.

"She's better. We just moved to a new apartment from my friend's house, and she was sniffing around earlier in the afternoon on a walk and was chewing on something, but I didn't see what it was. Whatever it was, it must've triggered her. Is the coach you mentioned here?" I ask, switching the topic.

"Yeah, he's over there." Bart turns to his right and points to Coach Thomas, surrounded by five or six people and engaged in conversation.

"Let's say hi before everything gets started," Bart suggests.

"Sure thing," I say nervously. My hands are sweaty, and I follow Bart through the small crowd to join the group.

As we walk up, Coach Thomas turns toward us. "Welcome!" he says with a big smile.

His name tag reads "Coach Thomas Sharon," with a smiley face.

"Hey, Tom, this is Joel, the sharp manager I work with from Hank and Harry's on Army Post Road. Joel, this is Coach Thomas," Bart says, introducing us.

"Thomas Sharon," he says in a deep voice and extends his hand. "You can call me Tom or Coach Thomas."

"Joel Edmonds," I respond, and shake his hand.

A few members of the previous conversation start a new conversation, and Coach Thomas and I begin to chat.

"Bart mentioned that you were going through some challenges and thought it'd be good for us to meet," Coach Thomas says.

"Yeah, managing my store is pretty stressful, and I'm finalizing my divorce," I begin. "I also went on a trip a couple of days ago to figure out what I wanted to do, and it was a nightmare. I feel lost, like something is missing. Can you help me?" I ask.

"What do you know about coaching?" Coach Thomas asks.

"Excuse me," Bart chimes in. "I see someone I want to say hi to." He pats me on the back as he exits the conversation.

"Coaching?" I pause to think. "Well, I played hockey in high school, so I'm familiar with coaching in sports—coming up with plays and running drills. With your coaching, I guess there's a lot less yelling," I joke.

"Yeah," Coach Thomas says with a laugh. "There's no yelling. It's a collaborative process that centers around co-creating practices to deepen awareness and supports strengthening your ability to empower your choices around what you're working on, like designing projects that move your life forward and developing structures to sustain motivation," he explains. "Tell me about what you have going on outside of work."

"Outside of work and the divorce? Not much. I have season tickets for the Iowa Grizzlies, and I have a dog," I say.

"If we were to work together, can you tell me what you are committed to creating in your life?" Coach Thomas asks.

"Committed to?" I repeat. "I've been listening to some podcasts, and they suggest journaling, so I've been doing some of that to address my stress. I guess I'm committed to figuring out how to be less stressed. And I'm determined for my store to be successful. I'm just so busy," I say, beginning to ramble.

"Hmm," Coach Thomas says, nodding. "If you picture yourself from that future place, what shifts in your environment? What does this version of successful look like for you?"

"That's a good question. I don't really know," I say.

"Would you say the same old habits that frustrated you in some way before are still frustrating you?" Coach Thomas asks.

"Maybe? I want something more than what I have," I say.

"Are you willing to step out of your comfort zone and commit to creating success for your life and your store in the long run?"

"I don't know where that might lead," I say with mild defeat.

"Would you like to find out?" Coach Thomas asks.

"Yeah, I would," I respond immediately.

In the background, I hear someone say, "All right, ladies and gentlemen, take your seats. We'll be beginning our intros in five minutes."

I look around for Bart and see him nearby. Noticing my glance, he nods and holds up one finger, signaling he'll be just a minute.

"Will you commit to taking action to create this possibility?" Coach Thomas asks.

"Yes," I respond. "I can commit to that."

"I think we may be a good fit to work together," Coach Thomas says, "but before we can begin working together officially, there are some ground rules. Life coaching is about engaging in what you want and creating life from a place of possibility. I expect you to do what you say you will do."

"OK," I say nervously.

"If you're serious about developing a meaningful purpose for your life from this moment forward, close your eyes and be still. Notice how you're feeling right now. What meaning do you think is missing?" Coach Thomas asks.

Still feeling nervous, I close my eyes.

"Think about what you're willing to do to uncover the answer on the other side of that question. If there was a door that holds growth and discomfort before you, would you open that door and engage with what's there? What questions do you have?" Coach Thomas asks.

"I want to find the process for figuring out what I want in life and to trust what feels purposeful and meaningful versus where I am now. I want to live with purpose in my life now and be successful. I want healthy relationships." I open my eyes, surprised at the tears that are forming.

"Joel, I am with you." Coach Thomas pulls a business card and a pen from his pocket and begins writing something on the back of the card. Handing me the card, he says, "Go to this website. It's my new registration site, and you'll find a short questionnaire. Think of it as the first step in your journey. I wrote the password for you to gain access to the module. Register only if you're committed to doing the work. If you agree, complete the activity, and we'll reconnect in a week."

"Thank you, Coach Thomas. I like that idea. I'll do it." We shake hands, and I head over to Bart.

CHAPTER 7

Departure

"Are you all right, Joel?"

I jump at the sound of Lucas's question, not realizing that I've zoned out in the break room. "Oh hey, Lucas," I respond. "Sorry I didn't see you there."

"Deep thoughts?" he asks.

"Hah! I came in for coffee and started thinking about a conversation I had this morning," I begin. "I met a business success coach at a networking meeting with Bart Honer, and I was thinking about it."

"Yeah, you said you were going to an event or something today. How was it? What are you thinking about?" he asks while grabbing some coffee himself.

I motion for him to sit down, and I lean back in my chair. "Well, a few of the questions he asked me are ones I haven't thought about very deeply. I don't know what I'm getting into working with him," I say, instinctively raising my right eyebrow and rubbing my chin with my left hand.

"Yeah? Like what?" Lucas asks.

"Like 'What are you committed to?' and 'What you are working on?' I don't know anything about this guy. I'm just sitting with it right now. My divorce will be finalized in a couple of weeks, and my mind keeps coming back to that and working in the store.

Hitting our sales target this year is something I want us to accomplish, but you know . . ." I sigh deeply.

"Maybe you could be on to something," Lucas says, shrugging his shoulders, uncertain of what to say.

I shrug my shoulders too. "Maybe I am. Either way, the emergency order will be coming in tomorrow, and we will be able to get George Martin taken care of. That'll help the store."

"Oh," Lucas immediately responds, like he just remembered something he wanted to say.

"Oh? What's up?" I ask.

"Kim was doing something to the order in the system," he says. "She mentioned trying to add supplies for the Garden Center to it and thinks she may have canceled it by mistake."

"Canceled it?" I jump up and rush out of the break room, heading to the office next door to log on to my computer so I can check our inventory management system. "It's not canceled, but it's pending," I say to Lucas, who followed me into the office.

"Whew," he exhales. "You mentioned George Martin's order, and it made me think of that."

"Well, it's still there, but why the hell does it say pending?" I ask. "Well, thanks for the heads-up, Lucas. We need to get this order in for George. He needs supplies by Friday for a new grocery store."

"Take a deep breath. It . . . it's going to be all right," he says, trying to get me to calm down.

I place my hands on my head and begin massaging my forehead. "That's easy to say when you're not the one taking one step forward and five steps back," I respond. "I'll call customer service and see what's going on. We need to get this shipment. There's drywall, hundreds of gallons of paint, and a shitload of drywall joint compound George's crew needs to get started."

"We'll figure it out, man. We got it," Lucas says, patting me on the back.

I pick up the phone and call customer service. The pending order is scheduled to arrive early Monday morning.

* * *

Arriving home after work, I'm greeted by Presley, who is lying on the carpet in the hallway, facing the door.

"Hey Presley," I say, rubbing her on her head and scratching her backside. "Did you have a good day, Pres?"

She jumps up and starts weaving in and around my legs, excited for my return as I try to scratch her all over. It's nice to come home and sit down after working a long day. I'm still running on less than five hours of sleep, but I want to start Coach Thomas's introductory questions to see what he's all about.

After taking Presley for a quick walk, I change into a pair of sweatpants and sit at my kitchen table. "All right, Pres, I'm taking the first step forward today," I say. I take a deep breath and log on to Coach Thomas's website. The password *COMMIT!4U* grants my entry after I create a username and enter my email.

It's a basic website layout. The landscape of a mountain range in the background leads my eyes to an orange oval in the center of the screen that reads "Click here to begin your journey." Immediately I feel a chill run down my spine. I close my eyes and take another deep breath, then click.

Question 1: What are you committed to in your life right now? What matters most to you?

"Hmm." I scroll down the page, curious to see the next question.

Question 2: What are you committed to in your life right now that matters least to you? What doesn't matter?

"Hmm," I say again. This exercise is more profound than I anticipated. I decide to dedicate Saturday morning to answering the questions. I eat dinner, then head to bed.

* * *

The next two days fly by. Saturday morning, I wake up just before six thirty. It sounds like all the small dogs in the apartment complex are outside my window, barking because the sun is coming up. My mind jumps to a random thought: picturing Angela outside walking one of those dogs. She originally wanted a small dog before we ended up with Presley. My eyes open wide in fear, and I jump out of bed, trying to shake it off.

I haven't been awake for more than five minutes before Presley and I get outside and head toward the fountains in the middle of the apartment complex. I can see a couple strolling, holding hands and paying no attention to their barking Yorkie-Poo as they make their way around the fountain. Romance is in the air, for some. Meanwhile, I'll be officially divorced soon. I hang my head and stop walking. *I want to share my life with someone I love too.*

A brief wave of sadness reverberates through my chest. After Presley finishes her morning dance, we head back inside, and I make coffee and sit down to focus on Coach Thomas's questions.

After logging on again, the screen pops up where I left off in the exercise. I reread the first question.

Question 1: What are you committed to in your life right now? What matters most to you?

I take a sip of coffee and look out the window, where I notice the couple now cutting through the grassy area behind the apartment building. I start typing:

> *I want my life to be the experience of a lifetime, with no regrets. I want my life to reflect that I was courageous and willing to begin the complicated, deep work that would lead me to a deeper connection in my relationships. It will show that I was willing to try, even if I came up short of what I wanted at times and faced difficult situations.*

Question 2: What are you committed to in your life right now that matters least to you? What doesn't matter?

Sitting quietly and taking another drink of my coffee, I think for a minute or two before writing:

> *I feel like I'm associating with negative people and stress all the time. Other people's opinions of what I should be doing versus what I am doing shouldn't matter. I don't want to keep trying to get what other people have. I'm trying to move on and not be like someone who looks like they have it all figured out. I want to do the work to address my divorce and what I contributed to the relationship and move on. I also want to go to work and not hate life. Going to the bar all the time and arguing about what's important to me is not something I want to continue to do.*

Scrolling down, I click on the tab at the bottom of the page to save my answers, and the website begins to load a new page with the next two questions.

Question 3: If life removed obstacles and barriers from your journey, what would be possible for you to create? Describe who you see yourself being.

"Who would I be? Hmm," I say out loud. I type into the blank box:

> *I would be the best version of myself that I can be. Honestly, I don't even know how I would do it.*

Question 4: List what you could do to spend more time doing what matters to you.

I think for a minute about what I'm already doing and then type:

> *I'm already going to hockey games, but I'm not doing much to deepen relationships. Maybe I can read about relationships and communication or meet new people. I'm willing to give focused effort and attention to each item that will lead me to the life I truly want. To be the best man I can be and show that in my actions. My goals need focus and follow-through.*

After clicking on the Save and Proceed tab, the next page loads.

Question 5: What can you give to move that from thought to action?

Drawing a blank, I stand up and walk down the hall and back to the table, lost in thought. Presley jumps up at the sight of my movement and, tail wagging, follows my back-and-forth pacing. I finally sit down to type:

> *I will not give to the point that I feel overwhelmed and become stressed. Distress is not good for motivation. Distress*

is not an acceptable result. Still, I need to get out and look for events to attend. I need some help with this answer.

Question 6: What are you spending "too much" time doing well that doesn't serve you?

Immediately, I answer:

Working sixty hours a week with a shitty assistant manager who doesn't care about the store's performance.

Question 7: What kind of person would you be if you were 1 percent happier every day? Think about how your actions impact others. Who are you around?

I'd be less stressed first of all, maybe even more focused and more consistent at work. My actions would show each day that I'm a person of character and honesty. I'd meet like-minded individuals who want to be around sound character and honesty. I would be the change I want to see in the world, and I would raise my level of integrity and be committed to do what I say. My efforts would be supported, encouraged, and rooted in leading me toward the life I want.

I feel a nervous energy in my chest and start to tear up after rereading my answer. Taking a deep breath, I get up and walk over to Presley, who is lying in front of the back door. She wags her tail, and I kneel next to her and hug her, squeezing her a little, like a parent would a child they love.

"I love you, pup," I say and shed a few tears as I continue to hold her. Presley leans into me and licks my face. After a few seconds, I get up, grab another cup of coffee, and click the Save and Proceed tab. I'm at the final question of the initial exercise.

Question 8: So, you must be ____?

These questions already feel like part of my new journey, like the first steps in moving forward. I'm admitting something I haven't told anyone in a long time. I answer the last question.

> *I must be committed to my recovery from pain and the emotional impact of divorce and connect to a community dedicated to the journey of living fulfilling and meaningful life experiences.*

I click Submit, and a scheduling prompt comes on screen.

Thank you so much for being committed to yourself and taking action to create the future you. Please select a day below to schedule your follow-up call to review the next steps of your journey.

I click on the calendar icon to search for the soonest availability.

"Well, Pres," I say, "it looks like Tuesday we find out what's next." I choose the 5:00 p.m. time slot and click Submit.

"Whew. Well, here we go."

✱✱✱

Monday morning arrives, and I get to the store around five fifteen. It's cold and dark out, and the wind is whipping around behind the store, blowing a light dusting of snow and garbage across the loading dock.

I pull out my phone and check the weather—32 degrees and 20 mph winds.

Sunrise still isn't for almost two hours. The one downside of my emergency order arriving for George and the Smart Renovations project is that it's on the schedule to come today before six o'clock. I call Kim, who should arrive any minute to help unload the semi we're expecting, but there's no answer.

I leave a message, "Hey, Kim, it's Joel. It's about twenty after five. I'm just checking to see when you'll be here. George's order should be here in the next ten minutes, and I'm just starting to prep the loading dock to receive the freight. Call me back and let me know when you'll be here. Thanks." I hang up the phone and head over to the break room to start some coffee for my morning pick-me-up.

As the coffee is brewing, I grab the snow shovel propped by the back door and begin to clear the loading dock and walkway, adding ice melt to ensure there's no ice on the loading ramp or stairs leading to the sidewalk.

Sure enough, our inventory arrives at five thirty via special delivery. I call Kim again.

"Kim, it's Joel again. It's five thirty, and our freight is here. You said you would be here to help unload freight with me, and we've got eighteen pallets—twelve for Smart Renovations and the six pallets of fertilizer and potting soil you ordered."

The semitruck swings around the back parking lot and begins to back into our loading dock. The sound of the backup beeper echoes in the early morning silence as the fifty-three-foot red-and-white trailer backs up. The smiling couple on the side of the truck is excitedly speaking with a Hank and Harry's employee looking at paint and color swatches.

I approach the cab to greet the driver, and he gives me a thumbs-up and rolls down his window.

"Good morning! How ya doing?" I shout.

"Is the coffee on?" he shouts out over a deep baritone voice blaring on talk radio.

"Yeah. I got a pot brewing right inside," I say. "It should be done by now."

"Wonderful. I gotta finish up some paperwork on this load, and then I'll be out, and we'll get ya unloaded. I'm not worth much until I get some coffee in me," the driver replies.

"All right, thanks. I appreciate you making it out here this early," I say.

"Oh. no problem, my friend. An early start means an early end for me." He nods and rolls up his window to finish his paperwork.

Turning to walk back toward the building, I notice a couple of the lids from the neighboring recycling and trash cans have blown open and walk over to help out my friends at the dollar store. Then I call Kim again. This time the phone doesn't even ring but goes straight to voicemail. For the third time, I hear, "Beep. Hey guys, it's Kim! Leave a message."

I say in a frustrated tone of voice, "I could use your help at the store. Call me back. I'll be getting started here in a minute. Thanks," then hang up.

As the semitruck driver completes his paperwork in the cab, I finally accept the reality of the situation. Kim isn't coming, and I'll have to unload this order alone with the driver. I walk inside the back door and head to the break room to get some coffee.

As I begin emptying sugar packets into my coffee cup, I hear the back door open, and the delivery driver groans when he sees the cluttered warehouse. It looks like it wasn't given much attention over the weekend in preparation for the eighteen pallets while Kim was in the store with Patricia. Even the freight we received on our Thursday order has still not been put away. Four pallets are half broken down and blocking the bathroom and part of the warehouse where the outdoor patio storage is.

"Somebody had to pull strings to get you guys this load this early," the driver says, breaking the silence and approaching the break room doorway where I'm standing. "At least I don't have to wait around at the shop to hear who's taking a huge load to the rendering plant. You know what a rendering plant is, right?"

"No," I reply. "What is it?"

"It's where they take all the remains and waste from slaughterhouses, recycle the animal fat and cartilage, and turn it into products that end up in food and other products."

I wrinkle my nose, making a stink face.

"The smell is just rancid in these plants," he continues. "You get a small piece of this stuff on your shoe, and you'll track the worst stench you've ever experienced everywhere you go. If you get any on you," he says in disgust, "you have to take a shower, or no one will want to come near you."

"Gross!" I exclaim, almost gagging at the thought of such a putrid smell.

"Tonight's my anniversary, and my old lady will appreciate that I haven't been driving around all day, sitting in that stench. It's the worst," the driver says, shaking his head.

"Well, thank you for making this drop for us so early. I've got a customer who's remodeling 36,000 square feet on the ground level of a four-story that will be the Grab N Go Grocery store on 4th Avenue."

"Oh man, don't you worry yourself," he says as he enters the break room and heads to the coffee pot, pouring some into his black-and-gold travel mug. "I'm slow goin' till I get my coffee in me, but I'm here. I'm doing." He says with husky-voiced jubilation.

"I'm supposed to have help. My assistant manager was supposed to be here, and I've called her a couple of times, but I don't think she's going to show," I say. "I'm Joel, by the way."

"I'm Carl. And too bad about your assistant," he replies as he pours creamer and looks around for the sugar packets, which I point him toward.

"Yeah, it is too bad. This all would've been here on Friday during the day when everyone was here. I had to make some calls to get it here ASAP. Still, my manager added six pallets of fertilizer and potting soil and ended up getting it delayed until today because of the order reallocation," I share in frustration.

"I wondered who ordered so much damn fertilizer and potting soil. It's 30 degrees. Ain't nobody planting outside right now," he says as he chuckles and sips his coffee.

"Yeah. I have a new assistant manager who is excited to gain experience, and my district manager insists that I give her more responsibilities around the store. I placed this order as an emergency for a customer remodeling the old Sherman Warehouse into a Grab N Go Grocery store and apartment building. All this drywall is to get him started. This dirt has nothing to do with it," I explain.

"Well, it's a good thing they shrink-wrapped the hell out of all that dirt. Could you imagine getting dirt stains all over those sheets of drywall?" he's joking, but I feel a shot of lightning down my spine of the terror of what if.

"I hadn't thought about that," I say. "It would be a nightmare."

"Well, it's all good, young man. Let me get my pallet jack, and we'll get going. We'll get you unloaded here," he says with a grin and refills his cup before heading out of the break room.

Just then, I notice the reflection of headlights pulling up to the front of the store. George is here early. *Of course, he would be early today*, I think to myself. I check the time on my phone again; it's 5:52 a.m. I take a deep breath. "We better get to work. My customer is already here."

***

I'd barely said goodbye to the delivery driver when I notice my phone ringing in the warehouse. I walk over to pick it up from one of the pallets of drywall and notice that it's now 6:54 a.m. The store opens at seven. I have six minutes to open the store, and Kim still hasn't shown up. George, still waiting in his truck, is calling my cellphone.

"Hey, Joel, it's George. What are you doing?" he asks me.

I'm tired and hungry, but I know he has to get this job started.

"Hey, George, I just finished unloading the last of the drywall and joint compound for the Grab N Go. I gotta run though. I've got five minutes to get the store opened. Kim didn't show up to help and I'm running a little behind. I'll see you in a few minutes, OK?" I say with a sense of urgency.

"Sure thing, boss! Don't rush yourself. I'm waiting on Junior to show up with the box truck to haul the drywall and mud for the first phase over to the jobsite anyway. I wanted to get here early with my trailer, in case we could start loading before seven."

"Awesome. Thanks for understanding," I say, then hang up and run to turn the store lights on and count the registers.

George walks into the store, bubbling with excitement, when I unlock the doors at 7:04 a.m.

"You look like a man ready to remodel a Grab N Go Grocery!" I proclaim with a smile.

"You gotta be excited while you can. Shit's bound to hit the fan at some point, so may as well enjoy the first day and go from here," he says, walking in with his fists in the air, then double fist-pumping.

"Hah! That's an interesting way to look at it, I guess," I say.

Just then, I notice Kim's car speeding through the parking lot and racing around the corner of the building.

"Are you hanging in there? It must be a long day ahead for you to be in the store to unload the truck already." George says, noticing my smile evaporate.

"How would you be early in the morning if you had to unload freight by yourself?" I reply. "It bothers me that Kim never called me back. I called her three times this morning."

I try not to complain but cannot help voicing my frustration about Kim's no-show. Just then she walks in the back door.

"I overslept," she says right away.

"You were supposed to open the store with me at seven," I say, with George standing next to me. "Since you didn't show for the emergency order, I figured you would be late," I say, shrugging my shoulders.

"Was the driver mad?" George asks.

"He may as well have been. Thankfully he was more interested in his morning coffee than about having to help me unload."

Kim walks into the office to clock in, then disappears into the break room.

"You're just going through a bit of a rough patch. Brighter days are ahead, young man." George pats me on the back, and we walk toward the pallets lined up on the loading dock.

I begin thinking, *I'm looking forward to working with Coach Thomas. Who do I want to be? What am I committed to creating in my life?*

CHAPTER 8

Permission to Make Noise

"Joel, come on. You know how tired I am and how I've been working all these shifts," Kim says.

"I don't know what to tell you. I'm tired, too, and I've been here since five o'clock. I don't have the energy to keep going rounds with you," I say.

"Why are you going rounds with me?" Kim snaps back.

"You barely work forty hours a week, and I'm working sixty. That's a twenty-hour difference, and you're saying that you're tired? You weren't even here this morning to unload the truck. You're short with customers and rude to the staff. I gave you the responsibility for the inventory order, and you didn't do it, so we needed an emergency order. It's hundreds of dollars the store didn't have to spend," I say.

Kim walks into the warehouse to try to organize the remaining mess around the pallets of inventory that are left over.

Just as I turn back to my computer, Patricia walks into the office. "Hey, Joel, um, can we talk?"

"Sure. What's up?"

She nervously asks, "Can I close the door?"

"Yeah," I say, and swivel around in my computer chair.

Patricia clasps her hands together and closes her eyes, inhaling deeply. "So, this weekend, I got to the point where I've had enough. I don't know how much you know about what Kim is doing in the store, but this last weekend, I . . . I'm just not going to work with her anymore. I want to put in my two weeks' notice soon. I'm looking for a new job."

"But Patricia, I need you. You're one of my best employees," I say, heartbroken to hear this news.

"I appreciate everything you've done for me, but I'm not going to deal with Kim," she says again.

"What happened?" I motion for her to sit in the chair at Kim's desk, across from me.

"Over the last few weeks, Kim has been a fucking hard ass," she says beginning to cry. "Every time she sees me sitting down, she comes up behind me and starts telling me what to do and insists I start doing something else. I'm busting my ass putting freight away, and sometimes I need a break. The second I sit down, she comes over, and is like, 'What are you doing? Why are you sitting? Are you studying up on products?' "

Patricia wipes tears from her eyes, and I offer her a box of tissues from my desk drawer.

"Last week she said to me, 'You're not on break. You're working right now. Do you see all that freight back here that needs to be put away? Put it away.' I'm like, 'Excuse me?'"

"Are you serious?" I say, shocked that I had no idea this was happening.

"She went into this tirade about how she's the manager and how she's been given all the responsibility to make things happen and do what she wants in the store, which in her mind is to crack the whip and get on everybody's case about what they're doing," explains Patricia.

"I'm showing up earlier to do work, and I can't complete everything I need to during the day either," I say.

"I don't know if you remember," Patricia says, jumping back into her grievances, "I took this job because you said you needed help."

"Yeah, I remember that day. You were a customer standing in line, and I was getting my ass kicked." I pause and shake my head. "Patricia, I value you being here. Is there anything else going on? Has this happened before?"

"I don't know if there's much to it, but this weekend I noticed Kim acting funny when she was in the store. She was outside with somebody she knew for a while on a smoke break. I thought she was on a cigarette break, but I didn't smell cigarettes when she came back," Patricia says, nodding her head and raising her eyebrows.

"What did you smell?" I ask, rolling my eyes at the revelation.

"Oh, it was a smoke break alright," Patricia says, giggling.

"Everyone assumes she goes outside to smoke cigarettes, but from time to time . . ." her voice trails off.

"Yes?" I ask.

"That's why I wanted to speak to you," Patricia says.

"Are you serious?" I ask.

"This is just the first time I've actually seen her, but I've been suspicious for a while, and Lucas told me about a couple of other times," Patricia says.

"What? So, yesterday wasn't the first time?" I say, surprised.

Patricia begins nodding her head again. "Yeah. I opened the warehouse garage door, and that's how I found out something was going on. I just wanted to get some air back here because I was sweating putting all the freight away. I tried to crack the door open, and she came running in, yelling at me to shut the door.

"The language she used and what she was doing—I'm not going to be around someone in a management position who yells at their staff. That isn't what I'm here for," Patricia says.

"What did she say?" I ask.

"Well, it was something like 'Listen, you didn't see anything, all right? Don't worry about what the fuck I'm doing out here. Why don't you just worry about getting yourself inside and put that freight away?'"

My mouth drops and my face is a mix of shock and disbelief. My chest tenses up, and I feel anger rising.

"Yeah," Patricia says and nods to affirm her words. "I was like 'Excuse me? Did you just say that to me?'"

"Well, that's not gonna fly in my house!" I say. "I told John her behavior was going to continue to be an issue. I'm calling him now." I pick up the phone on my desk and call my district manager. The call goes to voicemail after a couple rings, and I try to sound like I have something urgent to discuss.

"Good morning, John, it's Joel Edmonds at Hank and Harry's on the south side of Des Moines. I have an issue I need to speak with you about. Please call me back at the store. Thanks."

"Can you promise not to make a big stink about this in front of her?" Patricia asks. "Until I find a new job, I need to work here because I need the hours. Between you and me, I need to get the hell out of here and away from Kim."

"Yeah, I won't say anything, but I will need to talk to the district manager about this. A lot is going on. We're backward 16 percent for the quarter, and I'm going to need some help," I say.

"Well, I could be two weeks or a month, but I want to give my notice. I'm not working with Kim any longer than I have to," Patricia says again.

"Well, some days you might need to work with her. I still need your help in the store. You see what's going on this morning for George," I say.

"I get it. I'm not saying I don't want to be a team player and won't support you. What I'm saying is I'm not gonna show up and help her. If we're both working on the weekend, don't schedule us together because I will call out," Patricia says adamantly.

"I hear you," I say.

"This is nothing personal, Joel. My husband is fully supportive, and I've got my boy to take care of," she says.

"I'm going to email John at the district office," I say. "I want to be sure he knows we need some help." I turn back to my computer desk and look at the clock: 9:30 a.m.

"Thank you for not freaking out, Joel," Patricia says, getting up from her chair and wiping the tears from her face.

"Of course, Patricia. Please let me know if you see anything else," I say and begin typing.

RE: Store Support Needed

Good morning, John,

You've asked me to work with Kim and give her additional responsibilities around the store, and I have done just that. Now staff morale is down, and sales are in double-digit decline.

At 5:30 a.m., our emergency order showed up and dropped off eighteen pallets, partially containing necessary materials we needed for George Martin and the Smart Renovations remodel of the Grab N Go Grocery store on 4th Ave in Des Moines. This is a critical job for George and his crew.

This order was supposed to be placed by Kim two weeks ago while I was on vacation, but she claimed to be "so busy" and never completed the order. I caught the error when I returned and placed the order. Still, it was delayed until today because Kim added pallets of potting soil and fertilizer to the emergency order, using the manager's password you insisted I share with her so she could access our regular inventory orders. Also, Kim did not show up to receive the order and help with unloading as she promised, so I was here alone.

Now I've just been made aware of another issue I need to bring to your attention about Kim. I've voiced concerns about losing business, and I've expressed concerns about what's going on in the store and her behavior with both the staff and me.

We will have a huge day for sales today, but I feel I've got duct tape holding my staff together. I need your help. Please call me on my cell or at the store.

Joel

I hit Send and walk up to the storefront.

Kevin Ashland comes walking in. "Good morning. I brought some donuts and muffins for you all. How is everybody?" he says cheerfully.

"Hey! Thanks, Kevin," says Patricia.

"Yeah, thanks, man. What's the occasion?" I ask.

"Today's the big day with the order coming in. I wanted to get here earlier but got held up. I figured I'd catch you wrapping up getting everything loaded."

"That's nice of you. I appreciate the surprise," I say.

"Oh, you're welcome," Kevin says.

"Hey, George!" Kevin shouts across the store and into the back warehouse, excited to share the surprise. Using the nickname he's given George, he yells, "Smartin! Where are you?"

Just then, George comes walking in the front door from the dollar store next door.

"Who the hell is shouting my name in here? I can hear you yelling outside." George pauses in the doorway. "Who is that back there with donuts, wait—" he walks over toward Kevin to take a closer look, "donuts *and* muffins?"

Kevin and George shake hands.

"Hey buddy, good to see you." George turns to Patricia and says, "You know you're spending the big bucks when you get a box of donuts *and* muffins hand-delivered."

"My favorite!" Patricia says, licking her lips and pointing to her chosen morning indulgence.

"I brought enough donuts and muffins for everyone," Kevin says.

"Well, at least let me get the first one," George says and grabs one of the few chocolate chip muffins in the box. The aroma of fresh pastries and a chocolate blueberry delight mingles with the smell of hardware and lumber.

"Are you ready for this Grab N Go?" Kevin asks George.

"We're almost loaded up here. Joel was able to get the order here, and we're about ready to rock and roll," George says.

"Wonderful. That's good to hear. Joel's a good kid," Kevin says, patting me on the back.

Kevin walks over to Junior and Lucas, who are still loading the trailer. "I brought donuts for you guys, too, or would you rather have some muffins? I've got both."

Lucas jumps on the offer. "You know what, I will grab a muffin. I'm hungry."

"Wow, you guys are loaded down," Kevin says, noticing how everything fits.

"Yeah, we got about half of the drywall in here, and we're loading some of the mud to get it to the job. That way, the crew can get started unloading this trailer, and we can start on the box truck and get the remaining drywall and mud in there," says Junior Martin.

"Yep, we'll be in it then." George chuckles.

Kevin pats George on the back. "It's just the beginning, baby."

From the break room I hear Patricia yelling at Kim, "You're being a bitch!"

"Great, what now?" I say and head to the break room with Kevin and George not far behind me. Patricia and Kim are face-to-face, yelling at each other.

As I enter from behind Kim, I hear her say, "Listen, Patricia, you're a snake and a two-faced bitch. Fuck you."

"Hold up! What is happening here? What is this?" I jump in.

"I'm not a hard ass! You know I'm trying to get the most out of each of you," Kim yells.

"It's impossible to make you happy," Patricia says.

"I'm asking you to keep yourself busy," Kim says in a less aggressive tone.

"You're just saying that," says Patricia.

"I mean, I do actually like you guys. You're like family," Kim says, noticing the crowd standing in the doorway.

I chime in, declaring, "What is going on? We will not have drama like this in here."

Kim immediately gets emotional and defensive. "What is your role in the situation, motherfucker? What did you do? Stay out of *our* business."

I put my hands up, shocked, and take a deep breath, stepping back. "If you're having trouble in this store, it is my business," I assert.

"I'm happy," Lucas says, trying to be funny and chewing a mouthful of blueberry muffin.

"Come on, everyone," I say, "Let's get back to it. Kim, can we speak in the office?"

"Ugh," she utters and storms off.

Kevin chimes in, "Joel, have you called John about this?"

"I called him this morning and just sent an email a bit ago," I say.

Kevin begins shaking his head. "I don't know how to say this. Customers don't like coming in here and interacting with this toxicity."

I sigh.

"Just deal with it the best you can, kid, and don't get too worked up. I'll call John and see if I can get him off his ass."

"Thanks, Kevin," I say and head out of the break room and to the office for a heart-to-heart with Kim.

Walking into the office, I meet Kim's attitude.

"I saw Patricia coming out of the office earlier," she starts. "I bet you she has been talking shit. Don't believe what she's been saying."

"What happened between you two? What do you mean?" I ask, closing the door.

Kim begins to whisper, "I'm not supposed to say anything to anybody while she's in the store. Patricia's got a secret she doesn't want anyone to know about."

"Secret? What are you talking about?" I ask.

"Trust me. I'll tell you about it later," Kim says.

"Listen, Patricia's ready to quit," I say.

"Well, good riddance," Kim says.

"She mentioned that something happened in the store yesterday around a smoke break you were on and the way you behaved. Then you were late again this morning. Do you have anything to tell me about what happened?" I ask, giving Kim the chance to be honest. I feel tension rising in my chest that is not too far from feeling like I want to scream.

"Why don't you take my side and listen to me? I told you she was talking shit!" she yells. "What did she say? Nothing happened."

"The point is you were just in the break room yelling at Patricia and calling her a bitch, and she's yelling back. This is not OK. And I keep hearing that customers don't want to come in here and deal with you," I explain.

"Don't believe Patricia. I'm your assistant manager. Who knows what the hell she was doing before she came to the store? You should probably be questioning her."

"Listen, Kim, I'm trying to work with you, but you just called me a motherfucker in front of the staff and a customer. What the hell is going on with you?"

"Excuse me?" Kim says with a defensive tone. "So what if I'm hard on Patricia—she won't do what I tell her the first time," she continues. "I don't give a shit who doesn't like me."

"It's taken me a while to recognize that traffic has been slowly leaving the store. I'm not going to mention any names, but quite a few customers aren't coming in now. I think we're up to twenty-five or twenty-six now shopping elsewhere, and we're backward 16 percent in sales. Oh, and thank you for ordering all of that fertilizer and potting soil that we don't need," I add.

"Come on, the time for that stuff is coming," Kim says in her defense.

"If you go rogue ordering inventory, you will end up ordering material we don't need or ordering it earlier than we need it. We're not going to have enough storage in the warehouse. It was crowded enough this morning with the mess back there from this weekend. I don't know what to do to get through to you. I already told you I don't want to keep going around and around with you being late and tired again."

I sigh in frustration and rub my hands into my eyes, tilting my head back with a sigh. "Ugh, it's barely even ten o'clock." I use my thumb and middle finger to massage my temples. I'm starting to feel short of breath.

"I don't know what all this is about. I want something different for my life," I say. "Between the divorce and this . . ." I pause and exhale again.

"Are you OK?" Kim asks. "If I could get you to see it my way, you'd understand. I don't need you to tell me what to do, OK? I know what to do."

"I'm at my wit's end about all this. The way you're going about things is turning business away, and now Patricia is quitting." I get up and walk toward the door. "Your attitude is frustrating people, including me, to the point that nobody wants to deal with you."

"Damn, do you have to say it that way? You know I'm new," Kim says, taken aback by my honesty.

"Now you want to play the new card. It's too late for that, Kim," I say, shaking my head.

Kim stands up, staring at me in silence.

I take a deep breath and exhale.

"Fine, I'm calling HR," she says, shoving her chair and storming out of the office.

I click on the store email on my home screen, praying for a response and support from my district manager.

"Ah," I say. John did reply to my call for help. I tense up and click to open the email.

> *Joel,*
>
> *I told you, if you want to discuss this, please call me.*
>
> *You two will need to work this out peacefully and find out what you need from each other. This is not high school, and I'm not talking to Kim for you. Speak to her directly so she can hear from you what you need.*
>
> *John Allen*
>
> *Hank and Harry's District Manager*
>
> *Central Iowa District*

"Is he fucking serious?" I say out loud and jump out of my chair. I head out of the office, shaking my head in frustration. I see Kevin still sitting in the break room, looking at his phone, and I sit down and join him. There are a couple of donuts and a muffin left, and I grab a chocolate frosted glazed donut.

"How are you doing, kid?" Kevin asks.

"Well, I'm better now," I say, taking a bite.

"You look like you've just been in a tough conversation," he says.

I sigh.

"There comes a time in everybody's career, kid, when they find themselves exactly where you are," Kevin says.

"What are you talking about? There's no way this is normal."

Kevin continues, "It's not your responsibility to solve everybody's problems. You can't take it on yourself. You've got a lot of shit going on."

"I feel like what I want doesn't matter all over again," I begin. "Like with the divorce, here my choices and decisions are coming down to something out of my control. No matter what I say, or how much I try to do things the right way, it's always someone else's priority that's more important. Right now, I feel like I'm spending a lot of time on all this bullshit with Kim."

"Patricia isn't making it any better," Kevin adds, and I roll my eyes. "Working retail can be a thankless job some days. Take your time, kid. You'll get through this."

"Kim's sweet nature and voice appear so kind when she's in front of John or being fake polite. Then she'll call John or HR and complain that I'm being unfair. You watch. If you don't know her well, you only hear the pleasant, phony voice. If you spend any time in the store, you're bound to get the honest reality of Kim's attitude," I say.

"I don't know what to tell you. It's almost as though you're trying to force a working relationship that will never work," Kevin says.

"Patricia is already looking for a new job, and I know Lucas would go if he could find an opportunity that fits his schedule. I can't expect anyone to want to stay at this store. And apparently, John expects me to handle all of this on my own."

"You know, kid, it would help if you had someone or something else to look forward to," Kevin says.

"I need help, and I need to stop getting the runaround," I say. "I'm stuck."

CHAPTER 9

A Helping Hand

I rush into the apartment and see Presley sitting in the hallway, wagging her tail.

It's barely been twenty-four hours since the fallout between Kim and Patricia, and already Patricia has insisted on demonstrating her unwillingness to work with Kim by calling out and leaving us short a person today. Of course, the store was busier than yesterday, and it was nine straight hours of questions and phone calls.

"Hey, Pres. We gotta run," I say, grabbing her harness. "It's four thirty, and we have to go for a quick walk to the fountain before I talk to Coach Thomas." She weaves in and around my legs, panting in excitement.

The brisk walk gets Presley taken care of, and we head back inside. Taking off her harness in the entryway, I notice an anxious feeling. I shake like I'm shaking from the cold, but it feels like something else. I fill Presley's food and water dishes and sit on the couch in the living room to focus on my breathing for a few minutes and try to calm down.

I inhale and take a deep breath, holding for a second. Then I exhale, slowly counting to four. After the third time, I start to feel a little calmer, and I open my eyes to take a look at my phone.

"Nice. 4:55," I say to Presley, who is now aggressively playing with a purple and green dinosaur chew toy. Noticing me looking in her direction, she stops and looks up at me with curiosity, waiting to see what move I'm about to make or what direction to follow.

I walk over, pat her on the head, and give her a belly rub. After a minute or two, my phone begins to ring. I get up to answer it. "This is Joel," I say.

"Good evening, Joel. It's Coach Thomas Sharon. How are you this evening?" I hear on the other end.

"Pretty good, Coach," I respond. "How are you?"

"I'm well, thank you." I hear him take a deep breath. "How was your day today?"

"Um, a bit hectic, but when is it not?"

"What happened?" he asks.

"Well, we had a large order come in yesterday, and my assistant manager and I had a bit of a falling out. I'm getting to a crossroads with her, and one of my employees put in their notice to quit. So, I sent an email to my district manager about it, and I got a smart response, basically telling me to deal with it on my own. I've been asking for help, and today, one of my employees called out because they refuse to work with my assistant manager. It was a very busy day today," I explain.

"Tell me more about that before we get into the exercise."

"I don't know how much more there is to say. My assistant manager sucks, and my stress level triples whenever I have to deliver news to her that she doesn't want to hear."

"I think you wrote about this in one of your responses," Coach Thomas says, and I hear him shuffling papers.

"It's just that every day is stressful, and I'm not exactly happy in the store. Two of my favorite employees are about to quit," I say.

"I hear some resistance to your call and the gifts you bring to your store," Coach Thomas remarks. "Would you be interested in creating a new relationship with where you are currently and where you want to be?"

"Sure," I respond.

There was a moment of silence. Then Coach Thomas begins to speak. "Coaching is about partnering with you to create the space for change to become transformation in your life. Some clients have said that our work together was vital to them in aligning their actions with their values and was what they needed to stop blaming circumstances for how they show up."

He continues, "It's not like therapy. I don't coach trauma. We discuss the past, but we don't focus there. Coaching is about how we show up and what we bring into a room. It's about empowering our choice in the present and the impact of that choice moving forward. It's a force of creation and manifestation in our lives, especially when something comes up that blocks the way of us making progress."

"Wow, OK," I say in surprise, feeling a sense of excitement.

"Do you have any questions for me? Or is this a good place to begin our session?" Coach Thomas asks.

"No. You actually just answered the one question I had about what coaching was. It sounds all right with me to begin," I answer.

"So, I had the opportunity to review your questionnaire, and thank you for submitting that. I appreciate that you took the time to fill it out, and it looks like you put some effort into your responses."

"Thank you. I did," I say nervously.

"I want you to know that there is no right or wrong answer to any of these questions. This exercise is a tool for me to get to know about where you are and what you're focused on. Is it OK if I do some coaching with you today?"

"Sure," I say.

"Thank you, Joel. I'm curious about your answer to the first question, that you want your life to be the experience of a lifetime, and your willingness to do the complicated, deep work you reference. I take it that you're willing to try new things, and you mention the potential to come up short. Tell me about your relationship to the work you're doing now," Coach Thomas asks.

"Well," I begin, "I have so much pent-up anger from the assumptions that what I want doesn't matter. It sucks to continually hear that I have to wait out my scenario with my assistant, and then nothing happens. I feel ignored and not valued. After six months of trouble in the store and going through my divorce, I'm still in the same situation."

"What work do you feel you need to address?" Coach Thomas asks.

"When I got to the breaking point, and I'd had enough, I left my ex. I don't want that to happen with my job too. I don't know where I heard the phrase 'happy wife, happy life' the first time, but for some reason, it makes me feel like I have no opinion and that what I want doesn't matter. When I feel like what I want doesn't matter, it feels pointless to communicate what I want. I only end up in an argument about what's important to me."

"I recognize how defensiveness has impacted your relationships. I'm curious, what do you like about Hank and Harry's? What gets you out of bed in the morning to want to go work there?" Coach Thomas asks.

"Oh, I love that we get to hang out and talk about more than just hardware and remodeling, but mostly it's a paycheck," I say.

Coach Thomas thinks for a moment, then says calmly, "Imagine that your experience is going really well in the store, and Hank and Harry's is an enjoyable place to be. Everybody wants to work in your store, and customers want to shop at your store. What could you bring to this environment that makes it a place where you want to be? A place where you'd enjoy being—even if you have to make it up."

I think for a moment. "The store would be more organized and less chaotic. There would be no arguing with my assistant manager, and there would be more teamwork. We'd be working together, and it would be a profitable store. I'd enjoy being less distracted and not having to beg customers to come back to shop in the store."

"Where can you give your attention that creates the space to move this thought into action, to allow that thought the space to be in motion?" he asks.

"Well, I'm willing to try new things, and I'm looking for new actions to try or practice and develop. I want to help my staff achieve their goals too. I don't know about how I'll do this just yet, so I'm asking for your help on that. There are many areas I want to work on to improve. I don't know. I'm just watching myself so far," I say.

"It sounds like you're committed to staying at Hank and Harry's. Tell me about the vision for your career. Do you plan to stay in the store, or are there other places you're looking to step into?" Coach Thomas asks.

"You know, I've been thinking about being a sales rep lately," I begin. "I like how my supporting rep, Kevin, has many people that he gets to know as he covers multiple stores. It seems like he's got friends everywhere. His customers work all across town, and the way I'm starting to feel, I'd like to do something like that."

"What do you notice is stopping you from applying for a position like that now?" Coach Thomas asks.

"That's the thing—people don't typically move around much here. But I've heard that you can move up the ladder pretty quickly. I have no idea where I would even want to go."

"Are you willing to commit to realizing what's possible so you can find out?" Coach Thomas asks.

"I am. I just moved into an apartment. The trip I just took to Florida was the shit show that it was, and I'm not interested in going back down there and doing that again," I say, starting off with what I don't want.

"Where are you interested in going?" Coach Thomas interjects.

"There are a few places," I begin. "My brother is in Rockford, and I've been to Chicago. I don't know. I like having season tickets for the Grizzlies, and I'd like to be somewhere where I can continue to have season tickets. I didn't realize how much I enjoy getting to be around other season-ticket holders and the players so often."

"What if you had NHL season tickets? How does Chicago sound now?"

"Hmm . . ." My mind was starting to race. "I think we may be on to something here," I say.

"Consider listing places that might set the criteria for where you want to be. Where do you see yourself living? See what comes up for you."

"Thanks, Coach. I'll give that a shot."

"You'll give this a shot?" he responded. "Is this something you can take on this coming week? Could you make a list of places with a professional hockey team that you could get season tickets to?" Coach Thomas asks.

"That's an interesting idea," I say thoughtfully, rubbing my chin.

"Imagine seeing an abundance of Hank and Harry's stores with openings on your list, whether in Des Moines or a new place you want to be. Would that support your brainstorming?" Coach asks.

"Absolutely! I don't know if I want to leave Des Moines," I say, and pause, daydreaming.

"What are you thinking?"

"I'm thinking about how I could create such an experience where the sales process shows how we genuinely care about the customers, impacts service to our customers, and connects to the workforce," I explain. "For example, how can I connect daily with people, provide meaning and purpose, and train my staff to support their development and competency for this location? And why not promote Lucas from part-time to full-time, and so on? Maybe we'd have more employee retention.

"During in-store meetings, I could share something I'm reading that supports developing the staff and how we can come together as a group. Maybe we could role-play, and I could share stories of when I was in a different position, before becoming the store manager."

"Anything else?" Coach asks.

"I know that the results of this shitty experience will benefit me in the future, but I'm still not happy to be in this situation right now. I love that I'm breathing deeper every day, and for the last three days, I've begun meditating for five minutes. I don't enjoy dealing with Kim, and I feel like she's always holding something back. It just seems unnatural," I say, now on the opposite end of my swinging pendulum of emotion.

"I've been trying to teach everyone here how to be self-sufficient, and she doesn't care what I'm trying to do. Why is my DM making me wait for her to crash and burn? I don't need this drama," I complain.

"But you have it," Coach Thomas rebuts. "Joel, you have the power to choose to respond one way or another. What is standing in the way of you getting the results you want? What's your assistant's name?"

"Kim," I say with less energy.

"I want you to close your eyes. Imagine you're in a space with no cameras, and you don't have the obstacles you were just describing. Now describe being in a space where you find resolution with Kim.

Describe the vision you see. Notice what this opens up for you," Coach Thomas instructs.

"I'm asking customers to come back into the store, and they are. I can manage the busyness of the job. I am more at peace versus going 100 miles an hour," I say.

"I'm curious about something, and I may have a challenge for you," Coach Thomas says. "Let's say that a year from now, this obstacle is gone from the store, and you are in the place you want to be. You are even in a new relationship with the most amazing woman. You're in a beautiful place that fills your heart with connection in the community, and you get to go to hockey games all the time."

"What's the challenge? I like the sound of where this is heading," I say.

"The exercise I want to offer is around creating the future. Spend some time and think about that place a year from now that I described. If you could write a letter to yourself now from that place, what would you say? How would you be in that new place — in that new environment and new community?"

"Interesting," I mutter, and I begin rubbing my chin, my brow furrowed.

"I can do that," I say. "You know what, Coach, that sounds like a perfect idea. I want to do that!" I can feel the excitement and energy building and already bubbling up.

"Notice what you can put in your own words about your relationships or your work environment. Include even what you want to have in the future. What places would be on your list as excellent destinations to raise a family and watch hockey? What's important to you that you want to have in this place?" Coach Thomas instructs.

"Joel, this has been a wonderful conversation," he continues, beginning to wrap up our call.

"Wonderful. Thank you, Coach Thomas. I really appreciate this conversation," I say.

"I want to extend the opportunity to continue coaching for the next three to six months. We can follow up on things next week.

"My fee is five hundred dollars a month. With this exercise and your mindset and what you're talking about, your future possibilities sound incredible. I look forward to seeing what you create over the next few months," Coach Thomas says.

"Let's schedule a call for next week." I say without hesitation. "Does the same time and same day work for you?"

"Tuesdays at five are available," he says.

"Let's do that," I agree.

"Lastly, what accountability do you have in place to ensure that you complete the letter and journal exercise?" Coach Thomas asks.

"Accountability?" I repeat, caught off guard. "I can email it to you before our next call."

"Wonderful. You may also find it beneficial to review any notes you may take during the call or any insights you've picked up in the next day or two. Consider staying engaged a support for your progress."

"Ok," I say, nodding and taking note of the instructions.

"Well, Joel, I want to acknowledge you for taking action and doing this exercise and for being vulnerable and truthful with your responses. There's depth to you, and I look forward to working together."

"Thank you so much again, Coach, for this conversation. I appreciate it."

"You're welcome. Have a good rest of your evening."

"You too, Coach," I say, then hang up.

I look over at Presley, who's lying on her dog bed and staring at me. I smile and begin nodding my head.

"Yes!"

CHAPTER 10

Back in the Game

Walking into the offices of Merrick Law Firm and Associates, I'm in suspense.

"I'm here to see Gordon Merrick," I say, walking up to the receptionist.

"It'll be just a moment," she says. "Please have a seat, and I'll let him know you're here. Would you like some water while you wait?" she asks.

"Oh, no thank you. I'm fine," I reply and take a seat by the window.

It's been three months since I was last in the reception area of my divorce lawyer's office, but today the divorce is official. The smell of fresh flowers goes well with the painting of blue cornflowers and red carnations that leads to the office's hallway. For a moment, I get lost in the image of a prairie grass path leading to a meadow, weaving through the vibrant colors, before grabbing a magazine and flipping through a few pages. The melodic flow of baroque music calms me as I wait for Gordon. After a few minutes, I can hear his voice coming down the hallway, and my heart begins to race.

"Good afternoon, Joel," he says with a big smile, extending his hand.

"Hey, Gordon. How are you doing?" I say, standing up to shake his hand.

"I'm well. Thanks for coming in," he says. "How have you been?"

I follow him to his office and sit on the plush leather wingback chair in front of his desk. "It's a week earlier than I was expecting to hear from you. For some reason, I wrote down the twenty-first and not the twelfth," I begin.

"Yeah, no problem," he says, waving his right hand.

"It's been a challenging few months in my store, but I've moved into a new apartment and I've started working with a life coach. So there's some progress," I say, sharing an update of my last few weeks.

"Well, we're all wrapped up, signed, and delivered here," he says, pulling out a manila envelope from his desk drawer. The logo of his law firm is on the front, and he doesn't hesitate to open it.

"This is it," I say, taking a deep breath. *The official end of my marriage to Angela. Signed off by a judge.* Nervous energy radiates from my chest throughout my body.

"Yes, sir," responds Gordon. "I tell you, it's a hard road, man. Hopefully, things go well for you. I told Angela the same thing when she picked up her copies."

Noticing my sad look, he asks, "You OK?"

"Everyone's dealing with something," I say. "I'm OK. I just haven't heard anything about Angela since I left."

I look down at the paperwork, and there it is: Angela's signature. Immediately, I'm struck by a wave of sadness, knowing she'll be changing my last name back to her maiden name.

Gordon hands me the official copy of my divorce declaration.

"You know," I begin, "the therapist Angela and I used to see is also in this building. This is the last time I'm coming back here," I say.

"No hard feelings if I never see you again," Gordon says with a grin.

"Thanks," I say, chuckling and looking over the documents. "Is there anything else I need to do?"

"Go live life, my friend," he says and extends his hand.

"Take care of yourself," I say, shaking his hand again.

I make my way out of the office. Closing the door behind me, I noticed that my hands are shaking. As I walk past the receptionist, I'm holding back tears as I mumble, "Have a good rest of your day."

She smiles and nods. Like this is a routine she's been part of many times before.

Heading out the door, I take another deep breath. *Hold it back, man,* I think. I exit the lobby and head toward the parking lot. I can feel my chin quivering and the tears beginning to fall from the weight of the reality that my divorce is final. I get in the car and start sobbing.

I take a deep breath and another wave of emotion hits me, and I continue crying. There's no satisfaction here. There's no "fist in the air" celebration. There is, however, a sense of relief. I put the key in the ignition and drive back down Valley West Drive toward my apartment.

***

Saturday afternoon, I attend a West Des Moines Networking Group new members meetup at Tommy's Sports Bar and Grill, which isn't very far from my apartment.

It's similar to the last meetup where I met Coach Thomas. There's a table to my left to register, check in, and get a name tag, and the few of us in line nervously glance around. Everyone is here to meet new people.

Looking around, Tommy's seems like a nice sports bar. There are lots of tables to relax at and enough bar games to make an arcade jealous—basketball, air hockey, foosball, table shuffleboard, and all the usual bar video games.

About fifteen to twenty new members are already here when I arrive, including the event host and the sponsor, who are greeting everyone walking in.

"Hi, what's your name?" asks the young woman sitting at the registration table.

"Joel Edmonds," I say. She writes my name and draws a smiley face.

"Welcome, Joel. I'm Rachel. Have you been to an event before?"

"No, I haven't. This is my first time," I say jokingly.

"Awesome," she says with a smile and a laugh as she hands me my name tag. "We're glad you're here."

"Thanks," I say, affixing the peel-off name tag to my shirt. I head toward the bar for a drink. There's a group standing nearby, already in conversation. As soon as I get my drink, I jump in.

"Hey, how are you all doing?" I ask.

"Good. How are you?" asks a young and very professional man, who looks way too dressed up for such a casual event in a sports bar on a Saturday afternoon.

"Hi," responds a beautiful young woman from across the group.

I had already noticed her when I walked in and stood in line. A beautiful woman, with blonde hair, wearing a white cardigan.

"I'm Joel. What's your name?" I ask her.

"I'm Vanessa," she says. "This is Sam," introducing me to the overdressed young man. "That's Jordan, from Jefferson," she says, pointing to him in the group. "And this is Emily—we just met today."

"Hey," Emily says, and waves.

I smile and nod to everyone around the group.

"Have you been to many meetups?" asks Jordan.

"Actually, no. This is my first time. About a week ago, I went to a different event and met a business success coach. I figured why not give it a shot and meet other people to hang out with. How about you?" I ask.

"I've been to a couple. I met Sam and Jordan last month at one," says Vanessa.

"Well, this is a new member meeting, so most of us don't know one another," Emily adds.

"So, what brings you out?" Vanessa asks.

"Well, I work a lot, and I'm looking for connection outside of the Hank and Harry's store I manage. All of my friends have kids, and I've just gotten divorced," I share. "I figure if I want to get back on my feet and start meeting new people, this could be a good place to start doing something new."

"I'm sorry to hear about your divorce," Vanessa responds.

"It's all good, but thank you," I say.

Continuing the conversation, I ask, "So, what brings you out tonight?"

"Well, I work at Windsor Heights Dental and also have been pretty busy. I wanted to get out and start socializing a little bit," Vanessa says, taking a sip of her drink.

Sam chimes in. "This is my second time attending a new member meetup. I didn't vibe with the people I met the last time, and I want to make some new friends too." He adds nervously, "I'm glad you came by."

"Thanks. I don't know what I'm getting myself into. But hey, what's the harm in at least trying?" I say.

"This group is about making friends and having a group of people in the area to do things with. It's not like traditional networking where everyone is slinging business cards. They will highlight a charity event or business and try to generate support and awareness for local organizations," says Emily with a bit of adamancy.

"Yeah, it's so cool that they do that," Vanessa says. "Plus, you never know who you might meet." She gives me a smirk that makes me think something else might be up with her.

From the other room, I hear, "All right, everyone, grab a seat. We're just going to give a brief presentation about the group, and then you guys can play some of the games and have some fun and competition while we hang out."

We pause the conversation and head into the next room, where there is a smaller bar with the table shuffleboard and basketball games set up. I make sure to sit next to Vanessa.

"Hello again, everyone. My name is Rachel. Welcome to the West Des Moines Networking Group. So, to give you a quick overview, we're about connecting people. This group is for people looking for a connection, a friend, or a group of friends to hang out with, whatever. It's about meeting fun individuals with whom to explore the city or go to sporting events. Almost anything you can think of, our organization has a resource group that will support connecting you with other people in the community," she explains, pacing back and forth in front of the group.

She continues, "We also do some charity and volunteer work, and you'll see some opportunities for that later this spring. You never know where your connections might take you. So, when you meet others at meetups who might be entry-level or five to ten years into their career, imagine a connection or friendship a year from now, five years from now, or even ten years from now. Use each other as resources, because you never know who you know and how we can support one another. We have a spark that can deepen our relationships, and I'm glad you're all here. To kick things off, Tommy is going to explain about the prizes we give away to the winners of our competitions." She points to a man standing in the corner, and he walks out in front to replace Rachel.

Everyone starts clapping and cheering. I look at Vanessa and say, "I like this group."

"Good afternoon, everyone! My name is Tommy Brooks, the owner here at Tommy's Sports Bar and Grill here in West Des Moines, and I want to welcome you today. With Rachel here," he gestures in her direction, "we're going to host five games of competition, and whoever can get the most points at the end of them gets a $25 gift card to Tommy's, which will be good at any of our locations here in the metro. The second-place winner receives a $15 gift card, and for third place, well, we'll buy you a drink at the bar."

Everyone in the group laughs.

"All right, we've printed out some scorecards. We've got foosball, basketball, table hockey, bowling and table shuffleboard listed. Just tell me what your final score is, and in an hour, we'll see who has the highest scores," Rachel says, holding up the scorecards.

I look at Vanessa. "Do you want to play?"

"Sure," she says with a smile.

Vanessa and I begin playing foosball and flirting back and forth.

As we play, our conversation flows, starting with "You have a dog, I have a dog," and after bowling, sharing pictures of our pups at the bar with each other. At one point, when Vanessa is in the restroom, Jordan comes up and says, "Hey, it looks like Vanessa is vibing with you."

"Yeah, things are going pretty well. She's cool," I say, nodding my head.

"Good for you, man. First meeting here, and you already have a girl giving you the eye," he says. His comment strikes me as a bit odd.

"Yeah, I guess lucky me," I respond, flashing my eyebrows, unsure what his comment is about. After grabbing drinks at the bar, Vanessa and I walk back to play table hockey.

"Watch out!" I yell. We're banking the puck off the boards, and the puck is flying around. Vanessa's scoring on me, and I'm scoring on her, but she scores on me to seal the victory 5–4.

I feel so happy to be out. I've forgotten that I don't know many of the people I am connecting with. This is the type of activity I can come back to.

Ending the afternoon playing basketball together, Vanessa and I are holding our own but still in competition and flirtation. It looks more like we are lobbing the basketballs at the shoot-around game, laughing and giggling like kids, and the score doesn't matter.

As the final buzzer sounds, the score is 77 to 74, and I barely win. "Can I see you again sometime?" I ask, trembling as the words come out, but the rum and colas provide just enough courage to ask. "Maybe we can grab a bite or catch a Grizzlies game sometime? I had fun tonight."

"Yeah, me too. Sure, give me a call sometime," she says, and I take out my phone to add her number to my contacts list.

Not a bad night. I won a $15 gift card and Vanessa's phone number. Things are looking up indeed.

* * *

The next day, it's my time for a date night at Goods Bank Arena. Vanessa and I are lost in the shuffle of fans, trying to make our way through the crowd and up the majestic staircase.

"I'm so excited. I haven't been to a hockey game in a long time," Vanessa says, and I look over at her and smile.

"Yeah?" I ask. *Oh yes, I'm excited,* I think.

The stadium is full because we're playing Grand Rapids tonight and the Grizzlies have been doing well lately. We make our way past the ushers with the red vests and pressed black slacks. We get a smile and nod from our greeter as he checks our tickets.

"Welcome," the usher says.

We make our way to the main concourse.

"Do you want to play the 50-50 raffle?" I ask.

"Sure, why not?" Vanessa answers.

We head over to the young kids wearing hockey jerseys ten sizes too big for them who are holding the 50-50 tickets.

"Hi," one little girl says, "do you want to buy a raffle ticket?"

"Sure," I say. "I'll take six for ten dollars."

"Here you go," a little boy says, handing Vanessa the tickets.

"What is your fundraiser for?" she asks, accepting the tickets.

"We're raising money for the tournament we're playing in," the little girl says.

"Wow, that's so cool. Good luck in your tournament," Vanessa says.

"Thank you," the kids say in unison.

"Good luck," I add. It feels like Vanessa is walking a little closer to me now.

"Do you want to grab a drink?" I ask as we shuffle back into the crowd.

"Sure," she says, and we make our way over to the beer stand in the center of the main concourse.

"Oh, there's a shooting game over there we can play," Vanessa says, tapping me on the shoulder as I'm ordering our drinks. I turn around and see her pointing across the concourse at two plastic nets set up with the team mascot standing in as the goalie.

The fun-loving grizzly bear wearing the red Grizzlies hockey jersey makes big gestures, pretending to try and stop the pucks as a group of kids take turns shooting at the net.

"Yeah," I say with a chuckle, "that looks like fun."

"I'll kick your butt," Vanessa says, with the same smirk that caught my attention the day before.

"We'll see about that," I say and wink at her. "I've got a streak of winning since Tommy's." I pay for our drinks, and we head over to the game.

Five plastic pucks are set up, and we get our choice of left- and right-handed hockey sticks. The staff replaces a plastic practice goalie and tethers it to the net as the mascot bounces out of the net and returns to cheerfully walking and high-fiving fans around the concourse.

"Most pucks in wins," Vanessa says, lining up for her first shot.

"OK, good luck," I tease and back up, sipping my beer.

Swinging and grazing the top of the puck, she says, "Whoops!"

Whack, the second goes in. "I'm going to make the next one," she says with a smile on her face. Her next shot goes in.

"All right, nice shot," I say, cheering her on.

The fourth shot barely gets to the goal line.

"Well," she says in laughter, missing shot five in playful frustration.

I line up and score on my first shot. I look over at Vanessa. "Nervous?" I ask.

"Hardly," she says and sticks her tongue out.

Whack, my second shot misses the net, and my third shot hits the post. *Whack*, the fourth shot goes in.

"Uh-oh," she says.

"This one's for the win," I say.

"Is it getting a little intense now?" Vanessa says, joking.

"What do you say, loser buys the next round?" I joke.

"That's a bet," she says, her hands on her hips.

I refocus. *Whack*, the puck flies in, and I throw my arms in the air. "Goal!" I yell, exchanging a high five with the staff running the game.

"Lucky shot," Vanessa responds. "There were more people around when I was shooting."

"A bet's a bet," I say. "Let's get some food and head to our seats. We can grab that drink next intermission." I put my arm around her, and we make our way toward the concession stand.

As we take our seats, I can see Vanessa is excited. "Wow, the third row is so close. This is awesome!"

"I love coming to these games and being this close to the action. Maybe you can catch a few games with me this season?" I say, taking a sip of my beer.

She smiles at me and takes a sip of her hard cider.

As soon as the game begins, the puck is shot in the zone right in front of our seats, and a Grand Rapids player gets hit by one of the Iowa Grizzlies' defensemen. It shakes the seats and sends the plexiglass flexing back and forth, sounding like a car crash.

"Why is their goalie skating off the ice?" Vanessa asks.

"The referee is skating up the ice with his arm in the air, signaling a penalty," I say, pointing in the direction of the ref with orange armbands on his black-and-white-striped shirt.

A Grand Rapids player jumps in after the hit and grabs the collar of Grizzlies player Curtis Franssen and throws his gloves off. They both grapple with each other right in front of us, grabbing the sleeves of the other just above the elbows. Curtis drops his gloves and begins pulling and swinging, spinning both players as they struggle to punch each other. Curtis times the spin just right and starts wildly swinging, throwing a few uppercuts before losing his balance and falling over. The refs jump in as the crowd begins roaring. Everyone is standing, including the players on both benches, who begin tapping their sticks on the boards.

The crowd is going nuts, and people jump out of their seats, banging on the glass. Vanessa is screaming at the top of her lungs, and I'm clapping and cheering. Vanessa signals the beer vendor making his way up and down the aisles and buys another round of drinks as players from both teams on the ice pick up the scattered gloves and sticks.

The game settles down, and it's pretty close for two periods. At the beginning of the third period, Seth Jeffers, who is right in front of us, gets the puck and stick handles away from the defenders from Michigan when he sees the Grizzlies' hot-scoring rookie Tyler Ullrich standing on the opposite side of the ice, wide open. He makes a quick pass across the ice just before the Grand Rapids' defender can get to him, narrowly avoiding getting hit. Tyler catches the pass and quickly shoots the puck through the chaos of swinging sticks and goalie pads, and he scores.

The celebration erupts from the stands, and the Grizzlies' goal horn begins to fill the arena. Vanessa and I jump out of our seats and throw our hands in the air, screaming, "Yeah!"

The teenage fans in front of our seats run up to the glass and start slapping their hands, adding energy. As the players congratulate each other, Vanessa looks at me with a giant smile and her arms in the air, and we high-five each other.

As the celebration calms down during the stop in play, a guy dancing comes on the jumbotron video board, getting Vanessa's attention, which gets my attention. The guy is dancing hysterically and wiggling like a fish and chugging a beer during the time-out. His curly hair is flopping around while he dances to the music and patting his belly, really getting the crowd going.

Vanessa, with a look of shock and disgust on her face, mutters, "Ugh, really? I know that guy."

"Really?" I ask.

"His mom works at the dentist's office I work at," she explains, looking more embarrassed than finding the humor as the rest of the arena seems to be.

I look in the direction the camera is pointed and see that he's not that far from us, still chugging beer and dancing wildly.

Things were going pretty well, but now there's a shift in Vanessa's energy.

"Are you all right?" I ask.

"Yeah, I'm good. It's a close game," Vanessa says, trying to shrug it off.

The play stops again, and I look around the crowd toward where the puck has just flown over the glass. I notice the guy from the jumbotron walking down the stairs.

"Hey Vanessa, *wass* going on?" he says.

"Oh hey, Paul. How are you doing?" Vanessa says.

"I'm doing good. Did you see me on the jumbo?" he asks.

"Yeah, I did," she says with embarrassment.

"Who is this?" he asks, pointing at me.

"I'm Joel," I say and extend my hand to shake his.

"I'm Paul," he says and shakes my hand.

"Paul's mom works in the office I work at. We're friends," she says.

"Yeah, she gives me a ride once in a while too. Can you give me a ride home tonight? I'm probably going to leave in a bit and didn't know if you drove," Paul asks.

"Actually, I'm on a date with Joel," she says.

"Yeah, and I drove," I say.

"Oh," Paul says, throwing his hands in the air. "Excuse me. My bad, bro. I wasn't trying to creep into your date down here. I saw my girl, Vanessa, and I thought I'd come to say what's up and see if we'd hang out."

"Uh, no, Paul. That's fine," Vanessa says and turns away, trying to ignore him.

I notice red jackets from alcohol enforcement making their way down the aisle. One of them taps Paul on the shoulder.

"Hey, buddy, how are you doing?" asks one of the agents.

"I'm doing all right. How are you?" Paul says, oblivious that play has started again, and he's now standing in the aisle, blocking people and causing a scene.

They say politely, "We're doing well. Is your seat down here?"

"No, I'm up there," he says, pointing and slightly stumbling.

"Well, they're playing again. We need you to go back to your seat. You can't stay down here," the usher says.

"Oh, OK. My bad, my bad," he says and puts his hands in the air again. "Well, Vanessa, I guess I'll see you later," he says and starts making his way up the stairs.

"Bye, Paul," I say.

He waves and keeps walking.

"What's the deal with that guy?" I ask. "He wouldn't come over just because his mom is a coworker, would he?"

"Paul? We used to hang out," Vanessa admits with embarrassment. "He got a DUI a few weeks ago, and I've been giving him a ride to the grocery store and what not."

"Giving him a ride to the grocery store? How old is that guy?" I ask, turning around to get a look at him again.

"I told you, we're just friends. We hung out a long time ago. We're cool," she insists.

"Judging by what just happened here, I don't know if he thinks you're just cool. And based on where his seats are, he's probably been watching us most of the game getting close to each other," I say, looking at him as he takes his seat.

Vanessa looks over her shoulder toward his seat. We both notice Jordan from the meetup saying something to Paul as he sits down, still looking in our direction.

She turns back and says, "Well, I don't know what they're looking at."

I wasn't so sure.

CHAPTER 11

The Call

The next day, I take a shot at trying to smooth things over with Kim. I'm in the office catching up on answering store emails when she walks in to begin her shift.

"Hey, Kim, can we talk?" I ask as she puts down her purse and water bottle. "Like, have a heart-to-heart conversation to break the mold here, address the root problem around our communication, and clear the air about our working relationship?"

"What do you want?" Kim asks, sitting down her car keys on her cluttered desk before taking off her jacket and sitting in her chair.

"Well, you talk about how you are disrespected all the time, and it's typically a one-way conversation," I begin. "I feel like our working relationship is strained, and I'm not comfortable with bottling up frustrations when it comes to choices I have to make."

"Mm-hmm," Kim says, crossing her arms and rolling her eyes.

"Why are you here if you don't like being here so much?" I ask.

"I do want to work here. But how will I get experience if you control everything that happens and never let me do things my way?" she responds aggressively.

"If you want to be here and be successful, like your uncle, some things have to change. I want to help you develop skills to be a better salesperson and get promoted to your own store. Some of that process I know I have to own, but you're going to have to own some of it yourself too. Can we find some common ground?"

"Maybe . . . I don't know. I've been talking to Joanne, and we agree that what you're doing is bullshit. You should be giving me straight 7:00 a.m. to 4:00 p.m. shifts Monday through Friday and not scheduling me on the weekends. I'm the assistant manager, and I shouldn't have to work on the weekends," she begins. "I don't want to work all weekend. That's why I'm tired all the time. I'm here, chasing people to make sure things are getting sold and put away like I'm supposed to," she says, defending her actions.

"It feels like we're fighting against each other again. Do you feel it? How can we work together?" I ask.

"By you not pulling me into the office like this and talking to me like I'm not doing something right," Kim says.

"Listen, I want our store operations to produce profitable results. You don't need to be a hard ass all the time just because you're in a leadership position. I agree that if immediate action is needed, we can't let it go and have to say something right away.

"I want to work with you," I continue, "but it takes time to develop the skills to be proficient in your position and balance your workload here. If I give you too much to do, as I said before, mistakes happen. You could've had experience unloading a truck at 5:30 a.m. a few weeks ago, but that was another example of you sleeping in and showing up late. Why would I give you more responsibility if you can't consistently show up for your shifts or complete your current tasks?"

I get a side-eyed smirk.

"I don't know what else to say to you," I say, shaking my head and massaging my head.

The phone rings, and there's a knock at the door.

Kim responds, "Come in."

It's Joanne. "Joel, the phone's for you. It's John from the district office."

"OK," I respond. "Tell him I'll be a minute."

"OK," she says and closes the door.

"Kim, I'm going to have to take this call. Is this a good place to at least pause the conversation?" I ask.

"You're going to have to stop treating me like I'm an idiot around here. It hurts my soul to work on the weekends," she says.

"Hurts your soul?" I repeated. "OK, we'll have to come back to this. I have to talk to John."

Kim gets up and walks out of the office.

I pick up the phone. "This is Joel," I say.

"Hey Joel, it's John. How are you doing?"

"I'm in the middle of having another heart-to-heart with Kim right now. What's going on?" I ask.

"Is she with you right now?"

"No," I respond. "She just walked out of the office."

"OK. I've been working with HR the last two months about your situation in the store and your sales numbers dropping the way they are. I told Rebecca, the human resources manager, that your sales are backward double-digits and described what's been going on, and I showed her the paper trail you've been detailing, and she's determined that it's time for us to step in. We'll be there tomorrow, and we're planning to have a serious conversation with Kim about her future with Hank and Harry's," he says.

"OK," I say. I lean back in my chair and take a deep breath. "That's fine with me."

"Don't say anything to her. Just let her know I will be doing some store visits tomorrow and will be stopping by at some point," John instructs.

"All right," I say, pleasantly surprised.

"OK, see you tomorrow," John says.

"Have a good rest of your day," I respond and hang up the phone. *Finally.* I take a breath and try to hide my smile as I go looking for Kim. She's back in the warehouse talking to Joanne.

"Hey, Kim, can I talk to you again?" I ask, interrupting their conversation.

I see her mouth the words to Joanne, "Hold on a minute, I'll be right back."

As she walks up, I say, "I just want to let you know that John will be doing store visits tomorrow and he'll be stopping by at some point."

"All right," she says, shrugging her shoulders. "Is there anything else you need to tell me?"

"Nope," I say. I turn and walk away.

***

The next day, John comes to the store with Rebecca Armstrong from Human Resources. They look for Kim, and the three of them meet in the office for about half an hour.

When they call me into the office, Rebecca takes a seat to the left of John. She is very professional, speaking softly so as not to rattle anyone or crack the ice. John is passive, not enjoying having the spotlight play out in the store.

Kim is sitting in a defensive position, her arms crossed and a scowl on her face. She is definitely angry.

Rebecca runs her hands through her hair, brushing it backward, clears her throat, and begins to speak very clearly.

"So, Joel, it has come to our attention that there was an incident last weekend at the store. John and I thought it was urgent to address the matter and support bringing this to a resolution. We did receive your email, so thank you for sending that to John. Your patience over the last few months has been appreciated. I know it isn't always the easiest experience training a new assistant manager.

"Regarding your email, Joel, we can confirm that a customer spotted Kim behind the store over the weekend in question. They smelled something and witnessed her causing the questionable aroma. It was quite distinct, and the customer complaint time frame overlaps the timing of the interaction with Patricia.

"We have a zero-tolerance policy here at Hank and Harry's regarding drug use, especially in the workplace, and we've had a conversation with Kim here," she says, and nods in Kim's direction.

"We asked Kim about the incident, and she is very adamant that she wasn't the one partaking in the activity. We asked Kim to take a drug test, and she's chosen instead to resign her position as assistant manager, effective immediately," Rebecca says. "I want to allow you the opportunity to say any last words to Kim if you feel the need."

I look at Kim and say, "I wish we had been able to communicate better and that we could've worked together more closely. I still don't know what's going on in your world, but I wish you well wherever you end up."

"Do you have anything to say to Joel, Kim?" Rebecca asks.

"I'm done sitting through this. I'm done listening to you all talk about me. You don't want me to be here. I'm not going to be here anymore. Fuck you all. Shit." She grunts, jumps out of her chair, and slams the office door.

Rebecca breaks the silence that follows. "Our customer, John Ellison with Ellison Painting and Renovation, whom you know is a crucial account for Hank a Harry's, witnessed Kim and is threatening to pull his business. I'm sure you're well aware of Ellison Painting and Renovation."

"Everyone knows who he is," I say. "He's the customer George and Smart Renovations was competing with for the Grab N Go Grocery store so he could get into the remodeling market here in the city. Ellison is a major player. He can fix it, build it, and design it."

"Yeah, Ellison is one of the top customers in the state, and they are threatening to pull millions from Hank and Harry's because of this encounter," John chimes in.

"It just happened that the owner, John, was outside the store on that Sunday afternoon," Rebecca adds.

"I was trying to have more heart-to-heart conversations with Kim to see what was possible and figure out how we could work together, but this is where we've ended up," I say.

"Well, thanks for that," John says.

"Is there anything unfinished?" Rebecca asks.

"About Kim in the store?" I ask.

Rebecca nods her head.

"At this point, you've already decided that Kim's finally done enough to negatively impact this store and the other stores in the area," I say with frustration.

"My reaction wasn't as responsive because I saw it as an opportunity for you to develop your leadership skills and communication. I thought the scenario was supporting that," John says in his defense.

"My staff doesn't want to work here, and I'm stressed every day. I don't think that was a supportive process, but we are where we are, so whatever," I say.

"Well, we're dealing with it now, so it's probably going to take me some time," Rebecca says, trying to calm the mood in the office.

"I would appreciate support in the store, and if a problem is identified, can you at least speak to me about it versus sending an email saying that I'm on my own to deal with it?" I ask.

"Spend more time with the staff so they are self-sufficient, reliable, and able to manage some of the duties of store," John suggests.

"What else needs to be said here?" I say and throw my hands up in frustration.

"OK, thank you," Rebecca responds in her calm tone. "Is there anything else you'd like to say about Kim working in the store that would help you be finished with how things went, Joel or John?" Rebecca looks over at both of us. "Get it out now because we're moving on after this."

John begins to speak. "Joel, I want to thank you for doing the best you could with Kim in the store and for securing the Smart Renovations job. Your ability to get the orders placed and get material here for George speaks to your commitment to supporting your store and customers. You're even hiring new staff already. It shows you're committed to the store being successful and developing your people. I appreciate that you care as much as you do."

"Thank you, John," I say. "I've complained about Kim long enough, and I'm ready to be done talking about her. How long do you think it's going to be until we have a replacement?" I ask.

"We have some candidates in mind. We'll begin the interview process here soon. It shouldn't be too long," John replies.

"We're visiting all the stores today, asking other staff members about what it was like working with Kim in their stores and how it impacted their sales opportunities. We started in Grimes and then went to Waukee and West Des Moines this morning. We'll head to the store in Clive, then over to Ankeny, and end in Altoona. There has been some feedback that there have been noticeable changes at some locations. It really isn't just you, but unfortunately, yours is the worst of it," John explains.

"We hear you and thank you for taking on what you have and for doing the best you can with it," Rebecca says.

John begins again, "I asked you to speak with your assistant manager directly so she could hear from you what issues you were experiencing. I intended you to have a conversation and be able to resolve things. You can handle these things yourself. You're the manager here."

"Well, I began this job for Smart Renovations downtown, and I want this job to be done the right way for George. We're about to be busy with the spring season approaching. So I'll keep hiring new staff, but I can only train them so quickly, given what's going on. It would be a tremendous support if you could find me help," I plead.

"Know that you're supported, Joel. If you need anything, call me," Rebecca says.

As soon as Rebecca and John leave, Joanne walks up to me, holding back tears, and says, "I demand a transfer," and stomps her foot.

I sigh deeply. "Come on, Joanne. Why do you want to transfer?" I ask.

"What you just did to that poor girl—I'm not going to stand for that. I'm transferring out of the store, Joel, like immediately," she says, tears starting to roll down her cheeks.

"All right, Joanne. Do you have to?" I respond. "You've been in the store longer than anybody. You know the customers on this side of town better than anyone, and you're the most valuable resource in the store. If this is what you need to do for yourself, I'll understand. This hasn't been an easy experience for any of us."

Kim must've gone out and immediately told Joanne what happened before leaving the store, I think. Just then, I get a text message from Vanessa.

> *Hey, Joel, I'm sorry about what happened at the game. Paul and I are talking, and we're going to take a trip to Florida together to smooth things over.*

"Good luck with that," I type and hit Send in response.

I sit down on a five-gallon paint bucket, put my head in my hands, and start crying. *What the hell am I doing? Just when I think I'm making progress, now Joanne wants out. I've hired one person and lost three. I don't know if I can do this anymore.*

Later that night, I journaled:

> *I hate this hole I've dug myself. I want out of it. Fuck this hole and feeling sorry for myself. There is work to be done. Each day, take a step. What information do I need? What research can I do about moving? There's so much I can still do. Change is calling my name. Will I answer? There's no reason for me to be afraid. I'm doing the work and can't sit and wait for John to rescue me. I haven't fallen behind. I have moved forward. Just in a direction I didn't think I'd be going at this moment.*

CHAPTER 12

Return on Investments

The next evening, I sit on the couch, taking deep breaths with my eyes closed, preparing for my call with Coach Thomas. Today was another busy day in the store and the first with Kim, Joanne, and Patricia gone.

I can hear Presley on the floor, chewing on the multicolored rope chew toy I just bought her. She's surrounded by red, green, white, and purple threads she's chewed off. Right at five o'clock, my phone rings and it's Coach Thomas.

"This is Joel," I answer.

"Good evening, Joel. Coach Thomas here," I hear the familiar greeting. "How are you doing?"

"I'm doing all right, Coach. How are you?" I respond.

"I'm well, Joel, thank you. How has this last week been?" he asks.

"Well, yesterday, my district manager and the HR manager came through. They had a conversation with my assistant manager and presented a scenario to her. They knew she was caught smoking something questionable by a customer, and she quit. It's good she's gone, but now I'm short an assistant manager and two part-time employees. Another part-timer wants to transfer to another store because of what happened," I begin.

"What an opportunity for you and your store! Tell me, what do you see for yourself from this place?" he asks with an optimism in his voice that I find oddly timed.

"With everything going on in the store and Joanne leaving, I've been thinking about my life and what I want, and I'm considering transitioning out of the store myself to become a sales rep," I share.

"Nice! This *is* news. So, what do you want to talk about today?" Coach Thomas asks.

"Relocation and moving out of my Hank and Harry's store. I'm at a point where a change of scenery may be good for me," I say.

"You were so set on training staff before," he says calmly. "Has something shifted in your relationship with Hank and Harry's Hardware?"

"It took so long for something to be done about Kim," I explain. "I guess I'm still frustrated that I was stuck trying to deal with it all on my own. Now I'm even more shorthanded in the store. There's always something."

"If you were 1 percent happier every day for the rest of this week, what areas would produce an immediate impact that supports the mindset and well-being you would like to create?" he asks.

"What's 1 percent going to do?" I ask. "I'm getting my ass kicked in the store."

"Take a deep breath, Joel," Coach Thomas suggests. "Let's both take a few deep breaths." We stop and breathe together, holding for a second, exhaling to the count of four, and then repeat.

"Consider this the first step in your new direction, and it's all about momentum. First steps are often taken from a standstill, followed by the next, then the next, and so on. The space between the steps is like that 1 percent improvement. If another step follows each step, it's just a matter of time before you've got momentum and are moving further than you realize. What do you hear from that description?" Coach Thomas asks.

"My life would be more than I could ever imagine." I think for a moment, then answer again. "It'd be a courageous journey to make sure everything and everyone was a little bit better off because of what I brought to the table each day," I say with more clarity.

"What do you mean by that? How would you be on that courageous journey?" Coach asks.

"Um," I stammer. "Well, I'd be taking ownership of choices and not being defensive about how I respond to others," I say.

Coach Thomas remains silent, so I continue speaking, "I can see myself setting goals that allow me to achieve what's important to me and realize that I can deliver on what I said I would. And live my life with a purpose. I'm following through on creating and owning my journey."

"Is there anything you can see putting into practice today?" Coach Thomas presses me.

I lean back in my chair and try to get comfortable. "I could train staff on what to look for to be on top of orders and how to process them until they find their way of helping customers and filling orders. If I can train staff to sell, I can focus on running the store and give more attention to large customer jobs. I wouldn't be responding to as many customer service complaints," I say.

"There will be days ahead where some may still not be happy with what you've done, the progress you've made, or the life you're living," Coach Thomas responds. "I'm curious, Joel. Why is this important to you?"

"Why is it important?" I repeat, beginning to get excited. "I want my life to be involved in things bigger than me, things that reflect my values, and I want to be free of the feeling that I'm not leading my life. I want my life to be mine!"

Coach Thomas continues by asking, "What would support you as you make your decision around relocation?"

"We could discuss the costs and benefits, or pros and cons, of staying in the store versus becoming a sales rep," I suggest.

"Imagine that you're doing all the little things a year from now. You are still improving 1 percent every day and showing up in a new way in your Hank and Harry's store and in your relationships, and you're in the place where you want to be with season hockey tickets and feeling connected in your community. Where are some places you could experience this transformation if you could name a place off the cuff right now?" Coach Thomas asks.

"We talked about Chicago before, and I don't know, maybe Denver or LA?" I say, shrugging my shoulders. "Dallas?"

"Anywhere else?" Coach asks, jump-starting my brainstorming.

"I want to go where there is hockey, it's a consistent temperature, and I can be outside enjoying nature. Somewhere I can go for a run."

"Tell me more about what you're thinking."

I continue to ramble. "Dallas, because I hear they're pretty good with barbecue down there, and you don't mess with Texas," I joke. "Chicago isn't too far from here and not that far from where I grew up. Who doesn't want to live in Los Angeles and experience the West Coast? Denver is near mountains."

"I'm curious," Coach begins again, "what growth could you experience if you stayed in your store? What do you see yourself creating here?"

"Well, I'd learn from my mistakes, take a different approach to training my staff, and communicate more with my assistant manager so we're on the same page, and I'd ask for help. Another year would mean more time building trust with customers and showing that I care about them and my staff. I could sell and demonstrate how to run a profitable store," I say.

"That sounds like this would demonstrate your leadership," Coach Thomas responds.

"Yeah, I might be able to do that now that Kim isn't such a drag on the store," I agree.

"Suppose your interactions in Hank and Harry's Hardware stores came from a context of not trying to prove anything, and it wasn't about being right or wrong," Coach Thomas said. "The situation with Kim happened, and you're moving forward, and you care. How will you be now that you see yourself empowering your choice?"

"Hmm," I say. "I like that it's about what I can do to focus on supporting customers and the store. I'm looking forward to the opportunity to train the staff and reengage with them so we can turn things around from what Kim was doing in the store." I'm beginning to think of my situation from a new perspective.

"What would I get that would be different if I weren't trying to prove anybody wrong?" I repeat. "That's a good question. Maybe I would be coming from a place where I'm not triggered or defensive but more inclusive of the staff. Conversations could shift, and I would want to spend more time around them. Maybe I would actually enjoy being in the store," I say with a chuckle. "Managing this Grab N Go Grocery remodel has been quite a headache, and I have been stressed."

"You don't have to make this decision right now, Joel," Coach says. "Take some time to think about it and see what you notice between now and our next call. Notice what comes up about being in the store to prove people wrong versus serving your staff and customers. Consider showing up with what you bring as a catalyst for the store to make it a success," Coach Thomas suggests.

"I like that, Coach," I say, nodding my head.

"The chains are off, and Kim is not there to hold you back from making your store successful. You have this opportunity to show what you can do and be who you are now. What can you begin to practice this next week regarding that and relocation?" Coach Thomas asks.

"I've got an interview tomorrow with a potential new part-time hire. Maybe we can discuss how they might handle challenging situations and have a heart-to-heart conversation about my vision for the store and why I'm in the position that I'm in. I could ask them about what they are looking for—what's important to them. We could discuss how I could support them in the store while we're together. I can ask about what would make an environment one they want to be in? I'd like to have that as part of the conversation."

"Wonderful. Now is the time to live, Joel. Imagine spending your life engaged with the areas of your life that make you happy by being rooted in your values, and your goal setting supports your direction. Imagine the results. Can you see yourself doing something like that?" Coach Thomas asks.

"Yeah," I respond. "I hadn't thought about that before. Thanks, Coach."

"Well, Joel, we're at our time for today," Coach Thomas says.

"Thanks, Coach. This call has been a huge support and has given me a lot to think about," I say.

"It's my pleasure, Joel. You know I'm here to support you and stand for what I see is possible for you. I'm excited to see what comes of this moment for you. If anything comes up over this next week, feel free to reach out," Coach Thomas says in closing.

"Thanks, Coach. Have a good week," I say, and we hang up.

* * *

A week later, I'm still short-staffed. Surprisingly, customers are quicker to return after hearing of Kim's departure than I anticipated, except there's one problem—other stores are getting their assistant manager positions filled, and ours still hasn't. West Des Moines, Downtown, and now Grimes.

"This is ridiculous. I need help too," I say, as another email comes to the store congratulating another assistant manager being placed. "I went months with Kim in the store without being supported. It's been a week since she left, and other people are starting to quit—and they're being replaced already? What is going on over here?" I say out loud in an empty office.

Sitting here with my left elbow on my left knee, my chin in my hand, I'm stewing and frustrated reading John's email to the district: *Join me in congratulating so-and-so on their latest promotion.*

In frustration I pick up the phone and call John at the district office, and just my luck, he's in. I wait on hold for a minute or two before he picks up.

"Good morning, this is John," he says.

"Good morning, John. It's Joel from Hank and Harry's on the South Side of Des Moines. How are you?" I say, ready to unload my frustration and uninterested in how he's doing.

"I'm good, Joel. What's up?" he asks.

"I have an issue with the last three assistant manager announcements that just came out," I begin. "These stores are filling positions that were just vacated, you've already got a new replacement shadowing one of them, and I'm still shorthanded. I've been working with a new staff in the store, and I need help too. I'm working ten consecutive days over here, and I desperately need an assistant manager. How are people having positions filled? It doesn't seem fair to me, John. I don't understand," I say, projecting my issue and frustration.

"Joel, you've got to understand that people are moving around. It's like putting a puzzle together. Some positions are a better fit for what we already had planned, so we placed those people in their new roles," John explains.

"Sure. That's all fine and dandy. But what about this store? Are my customers not important?" I retort.

"I'm not saying that," John claims in his defense.

I state my issue again as if now John will understand my staffing issue. "You were here when Kim quit. I lost my assistant manager, Joanne, my longest-tenured employee, transferred to Altoona because of how things went down with Kim, and Patricia found a new job."

"Joel, you have to hire part-time help. I'll keep searching for a candidate to fill your assistant manager vacancy," John says calmly, not following my frustration.

"What are you waiting for?" I ask directly.

"To be honest, Joel, I made an offer to a candidate last week, but they declined the offer to be placed on the South Side. I have an interview scheduled with a couple of potential candidates that could start soon," John begins, and my heart begins to lift from my pit of frustration. "I've got someone in mind, but they're just about to get into the training program. It's still going to be another seven weeks before they'd be capable of handling the bare minimum assistant manager responsibilities."

"Are you saying I have to wait two months for an assistant manager?" I ask in disbelief.

"You may have to because we don't have the help," he admits.

"We're going into the busiest season here, and I was already working close to sixty hours a week when Kim was here," I say, placing my hand on my forehead and massaging my temples.

"You'll have to hire more part-time help. There's no way around that," John says, trying to calm me down. "Take a deep breath, Joel."

"I've hired eight people over the last year for the same positions and couldn't keep them around because of Kim. I've got the job openings posted and have been reaching out to customers inviting them back into the store. I'm in the office at six in the morning doing assistant manager paperwork. You're asking me to go into the busy season for two months like this?" I start shaking my head. "This is ridiculous."

Kevin walks into the office, talking on his cell phone to a customer.

John says, "Joel, I understand that you're frustrated. It's just going to take some time."

"If I need to host a new management trainee in my store to fill the position, I'm willing to do so," I say. I'm visibly frustrated now. "Please let me know how soon we can fill this position," I say.

"Focus on building your team up to the best they can be," John continues. "You'll be OK, Joel. We'll speak again when I have more information."

"I don't like this, John, but it is what it is," I say, resigned that nothing has changed from making this call. "Let me know when you hear anything more."

"I will, Joel. Have a good day," John says.

"You too," I say, hanging up the phone and rolling my eyes.

"Did you hear that downtown is being assigned an assistant manager?" Kevin asks.

"Yeah, I just called the district office. John says he offered them the assistant manager position here last week, and they turned it down. I have to hire more part-time help in the meantime," I say, shaking my head. "I'm grateful you were willing to go through that with

Kim. Most other sales reps stopped coming by, but you kept supporting the store, especially with George and Smart Renovations. I appreciate it. You could've taken that job to the store downtown to avoid Kim altogether."

"Well, it's not like I didn't ask George if he wanted to do that," he begins.

I give him a look in surprise.

"I had to give him options," Kevin continues. "George is loyal to you and this store. He's been building up the credibility of his account for the last seven or eight years now, and this job is his first significant opportunity to remodel grocery stores in large commercial spaces. I'm glad that it's still coming out of South Side.

"I appreciate you, kid. You know I've always got your back. You're trying your best and are working hard. This store is like my home, too, and I want you all to succeed," he says, patting me on the back.

"This is also where I sweated and worked my ass off for years. Shit, I got my come up from here too," Kevin admits with nostalgia.

"On my coaching call this week, Coach Thomas and I discussed how I have an opportunity to shift how I'm being about working in the store to improve the environment. I'm considering applying for a position somewhere that is a new opportunity to live the life of my dreams, though. Each day this seems less like this is the place where I want to stay," I admit.

"Yeah? Funny you should mention that. Did you know there are positions open in Seattle? Like three or four stores and supporting sales rep positions," Kevin shares. "I was in Waukee this morning, and their assistant manager was poking around job postings to see what was out there because of all of the assistant manager promotions lately."

"I had no idea. I just started looking in the Chicago area," I respond.

"Would you consider being out in Seattle?" he asks.

I turn to my computer to pull up the open job postings for Hank and Harry's, and search *Seattle*. I look over one of the open position's requirements and read the job responsibilities description, imagining what Seattle would be like. I look over at my Iowa Grizzlies giveaway magnet schedule and they only have seven home games left in the regular season.

"You know, I'd like being somewhere with mountains or a lake nearby or some unique feature different from the hills and cornfields out here," I say, giving the idea a brief thought. "I don't mind the rain. Spring is my favorite time of year."

I begin massaging my forehead again, wrinkling the skin, and sigh. "I have been getting my ass kicked all week. I'll look into this," I say.

"You thought you had it bad before," Kevin jokes.

"I don't think John seems very eager about placing an assistant here, which is why I called him. I'm going to be putting in close to seventy hours this week," I say.

"Yeah, that sucks," Kevin says, nodding in agreement.

"I can get stuff done, but I have to get here at like six in the morning, and I've been here until almost eight o'clock every night since last week," I share. "I'm getting sick of every day being a struggle here. I enjoy working with the new staff I hired to replace

Patricia and Joanne. It's only been a couple of days with Wyatt, and Roselynn is picking up pretty quickly. Roselynn has sold a couple of Master 10 riding lawnmowers that Kim never attempted to sell or even asked anybody if they were interested in purchasing."

"Yeah? Those are like two or three grand each. Good for her," Kevin says in surprise, nodding his head.

"I was starting to doubt that I could train anyone around the sales process, but watching them both over the last two weeks alone shows that something is happening."

"Don't sell yourself short, kid. Kim didn't have ears to hear what you were saying," Kevin responds. "It must feel good to have staff who listens to your suggestions now."

"It does," I respond. I've been journaling, listening to podcasts, and working with Coach Thomas for a couple months now, and I'm noticing a shift in my perspective when it comes to working with the staff. I want to focus on building them up to be the best. Not just in the store, but where it matters to them, at home or with whatever they've got going on. I don't want another situation like Kim's.

"Roselynn is good with homeowners and making home floral decor arrangements," I continue. "We were doing a role-play, and she had an idea to reengage customers by talking about flowers and the upcoming spring changes. She suggested matching bags of potting soil with types of flowers and creating gardening sets with tools and plant food as a way to boost sales. She even made this decorative springtime truck painting on the blackboard in the store lobby that reads 'Spruce up your home with Hank and Harry's this spring.' Our 'Home and Garden Starter Kit,' she calls it."

I lead Kevin out of the office and into the warehouse, where we have stored a few of the starter kits.

"I was going to ask who decorated that blackboard in the lobby. It sounds like you're on your way with the new staff, kid. Very creative." He looks intently at the organized bags of plant food, flowerpots, assorted tools, and flower bulbs.

"Well, hey," Kevin says in transition, "I wanted to check on you to see how you were doing and see if you wanted to talk before I head home."

"It's three o'clock. You're heading home now?" I ask, looking at the clock on my phone.

"What can I say? That's why I became a rep. I get my shit done, and then I go home," he says. "Anything else going on?"

"Yeah," I say with a chuckle, "Vanessa texted me today, like, 'What's up?'"

"Did she feel the need to reach out to you?" he asks with confusion.

"She has a man to go to Florida with. I don't have time for drama," I say, scrolling through her texts on my phone and shaking my head.

"Yeah, friendzone her, man," he says, as we make our way up to the storefront.

"Well, I've been thinking now that Angela and I are officially divorced, and after dating Vanessa, I want to be proud of the next relationship I'm in. I'm not trying to be some man on the side over here," I say.

"I hear you. How's your life coach?" Kevin asks.

"It's been incredible. We've been completing exercises and engaging with areas I see myself developing. I feel like we're making a lot of progress," I say.

"You're on to something, Joel. I had no idea you could be supported by a life coach like this, much less work with a coach looking at what you want and taking action to create it," Kevin admits.

"Thanks," I say.

As we approach the front entryway, Kevin says, "If I had a chance to do it over again, I'd probably relocate if I were in your shoes. All this bullshit you've had to deal with involving John—I wouldn't let that fly. I'd call him out to his face, but I've known him for fifteen years. Don't get me wrong—I love this community and would never leave now that I've set my roots here with my wife and kids. You have no relationship tying you here, and you could post to a new position anywhere. You are in a pretty good spot, Joel."

"Thanks, Kevin. I appreciate that," I say, and we shake hands and hug.

"Yeah, take care of yourself. And thank you for doing everything you can to support this store," Kevin says, walking out.

"Thanks, Kevin," I say and wave. "I'll see you later."

I walk up to the front counter, where the single-gallon paint shakers are busy mixing a few gallons of paint. Wyatt is processing transactions with Roselynn, who is trying to color match a decorative pillow that a customer had brought in. Wyatt is trying his best on day three.

My phone's text message alert sounds, diverting my attention as I get up to the counter, and I pull out my phone to see it's from Evan.

RE: Backyard BBQ at Evan and Mel's. The weather is warming up! Bring a beverage and something for the grill!

That sounds like a good time with friends after working this long stretch. My friends mostly all have kids now, and I don't see any of them that often. As I type my response, "Count me in," I hear a customer, Gil Roche, freaking out.

"I painted this fucking building the wrong color!" he yells.

I walk over. "Hey, Gil, what's going on?" I ask.

"That Patricia made the wrong damn color for that house in Beaverdale," he says angrily.

"When was this? Before she left?" I ask, raising an eyebrow.

"She left?" he asks with a confused look.

"Yeah. She's been gone for like two weeks, man. How are you just realizing now that you painted the wrong color? Do you have a receipt?" I ask.

He hands me a crumpled wad of papers.

"I spent a week painting the wrong color on six buildings," he yells.

As I look at the receipts in the bunch, I notice that the Hank and Harry's receipt is from the store downtown.

"This is not the correct receipt," I say and walk to a register. I begin typing, trying to find a transaction to confirm his sale.

Gil continues to get upset and starts yelling, "I just wanted to get this done so we could be done and go. Can you just give me the gallons? Kim would hook me up."

I respond, "Gil, I don't see any documentation that you bought that paint here. And I'm not going to give you gallons because you claim there's a problem with a color two weeks after you bought it."

"Do you know how much I spend here? Six figures. Is the manager here?" he demands.

"I am the manager," I say, with a head tilt and eyebrow raise.

"This store has piss-poor service," he says, slamming his hand on the counter and turning to storm out.

I think to myself, *Why not get out of this store?*

I turn to Wyatt and ask, "Are you alright?"

"I asked him what happened, and he started yelling at me when I told him Kim wasn't here," he says in a shaky new baritone.

"Well, that's no good. I've got your back. Let me know if you see anyone trying something like this again. No one needs to be treated that way," I say and head back to the office.

"Will do," Wyatt and Roselynn both respond.

The screensaver disables as I sit at my desk, and I see the Seattle Sales Rep job posting is still pulled up.

"Hmm," I mutter out loud. *What are you waiting for?*

I click on the posting and apply.

On my car ride home, I hear a commercial on an episode of The Personal Development Podcast.

> I don't know if you've heard about this yet, but we are launching our first-ever Four-Day Challenge on The Personal Development Podcast. Now, this is unlike any other

challenge you've experienced before. This Four-Day Challenge consists of four exercises. Engage with the exercises and our online community each week and be supported as you integrate your results. Immerse yourself in the experience and join us at The Personal Development Podcast website to learn more about the first challenge today. It will stretch your comfort zone, improve relationships, and call forward your best self. Are you struggling to figure out what you want in your life and where you want to be? How about supporting a developing purpose and meaning in your life?

Over the next month, experience what is possible for you in your life. With the Four-Day Challenge, you will not just change your life but transform it. Join us here at The Personal Development Podcast, where we take our personal development seriously. Join a community of individuals like yourself and experience what's possible for you.

"Hmm, that sounds interesting," I say, intrigued by the commercial.

Looking for support after my divorce and the possibility of relocation, I register when I get home. I'm ready for the first challenge.

Day one is a video. I click on play and begin to watch.

> The first challenge is to record a video, up to two minutes long, of a pain point in your life you wish you had support around that you haven't shared with anyone else. What are you struggling with and working on? Be supported in this community of The Personal Development Podcast.

Taking a shot in the dark, I begin recording, and for a minute and forty-six seconds, I share from my heart.

"Good evening, my name is Joel Edmonds. I'd say that right now, my most significant pain point is that I'm starting to recognize that I put the wants and desires of others before my own and what's important to me, and I guess I haven't spent a lot of time thinking about what it is that I want.

"One of my employees was let go recently, and part of my issue is not having help to replace her. What can I do next? I feel stuck working in the store I'm managing. I'm looking for something to grow into. I want to be more in tune with what's important to me and do something different to create new possibilities in my life that reflect my values. It doesn't seem like my current position is being supported, and I don't feel like I've experienced much professional development—or personal development, for that matter. So, I'm considering a transfer or applying for a new position, but I don't know.

"The point is," I continue, "I'm putting effort into this transition and figuring out what's important to me. Most importantly, I'm doing something about creating that possibility in my reality.

"If I stay in the store and continue repeating the same issues . . . I don't know. There could be a benefit there too. Right now, this is my most significant pain point. This is where I'm stuck—figuring out if I'm staying in my current position or if I'm seriously considering moving to Seattle. I want to figure this out. Thank you for listening."

CHAPTER 13

In a New Way

On the Saturday of the barbecue, it's pouring rain outside. Around nine thirty in the morning, I get a text from Evan.

Change of plans with the weather. We're moving the BBQ to next weekend.

It's been a week since I applied for the sales rep position in Seattle, and I haven't heard anything about an interview. I toss my cell phone on the kitchen table and start making some coffee. It's the perfect opportunity to check out week two's challenge from The Personal Development Podcast.

As I get the coffeepot started, I hear Presley snoring in the other room, lying in her spot in front of the back door. The rainwater pouring off the deck above my concrete patio slab is a steady, soothing sound. I walk back into the dining area, sit at the table, and log on to The Personal Development Podcast website. I haven't been on the site since I registered and uploaded the video. It's been ten consecutive days of working, with many thirteen- or fourteen-hour days, counting the commute.

The simple-looking website pulls up with a clean white header contrasting the black, green, and brown outdoor-themed website. I click on the Four-Day Challenge tab on the header and enter my username and password.

Day two is a written-exercise challenge, and a video begins to play explaining the instructions.

Today we're going to experiment with a purpose. Whose purpose? Yours. This challenge is to live in alignment with your values. What are you standing for? What are you taking a stand against? Decide who you will be when life happens with this values exercise.

Think from the perspective of already being where you want to be, not the past you're coming from. Take thirty minutes and list your values as you identify them from that place. This exercise consists of three sets of questions. Let's take a look at where change is possible for you.

I click on the tab to proceed to the next page and start the exercise.

Question 1: Write down your judgments that are out of alignment with your values and notice what you consider impossible for your life. Do you notice problems with others? Do you see a possibility in your community to live and thrive?

I begin writing:

> *I'm resentful for prioritizing only living for what my ex-wife felt was necessary. Carrying shame for not being good enough or financially responsible enough to be trusted in my marriage hurts to admit. And my old assistant getting the benefit of the doubt and all the second chances, while I got no support when I asked for it while she was chasing business out of the store makes me angry to now hear I have to wait two months for a new assistant manager.*
>
> *I had a problem with Vanessa for leading me on while dating some other guy. It's possible to start over in this community, but I've already been here and done that. If I'm going to start*

over, why not do it in a place where I can thrive and enjoy a change of scenery?

I click the Save and Continue button and proceed to question two.

Question 2: If you do your best work and show up fully present and untriggered in your environment, what actions demonstrate a transformation for you and those around you that are in alignment with your values?

I take a moment to think before answering.

I show up open and willing to do new challenges. I complete one thing every day that is a priority. I am paying attention to the environment I want to be in and the networks I want to be part of. I am designing my life versus reacting to it, expanding myself, and developing a growth mindset. I realize that sometimes the promised land looks different than expected. This will be no less than what I needed to experience.

Moving on to the final question, I proceed to the next page.

Question 3: What will happen to your network or community if you don't do the work to live your life with consistency around your values?

I'll miss opportunities to collaborate and connect with others around something meaningful. I won't lead by example or establish relationships and connections in the store. I won't be developing my staff.

This gives me an idea to try something. It's a shot in the dark, but if I can find the hiring manager's email in the sales rep's company directory, I can send them an email because I still haven't heard anything. I begin researching for a contact phone number and, after twenty minutes, decide to call a store in Seattle. It's the perfect opportunity to take action and demonstrate my commitment to creating something new.

I look up the closest store to the new territory and dial the number I find online. After three rings, I hear a familiar greeting, "Hank and Harry's Hardware, this is Jason. How can I help you?"

"Yeah, my name is Joel Edmonds, and I work at Hank and Harry's in Des Moines, Iowa. This might be a random question, but I'm trying to find a phone number or email address for Grant Holzman," I say. "I'm considering applying for a sales rep territory in the area, and I wanted to send an email and reach out to introduce myself."

"Wait a second. Let me see if I can find that," Jason responds.

After I'm on hold for about a minute, he comes back on. "Yeah, I've got a phone number and email address here for Grant. You got a pen?"

"Yeah," I say, reaching for one.

"His phone number is (425) 515-1035, and his email address is Gholzman@H&H.com."

"Sweet, thank you," I say excitedly. "I have another question. What do you like about Seattle? I see there are a lot of open positions out there. Is something going on out there I should be concerned about?"

"Oh no, it's not that. We're expanding quite a bit. Four or five new stores are opening, each with a sales rep territory to support them. I love it out here. It's such an awesome community, and the stores work together. It feels like a family. Honestly, this district has a strong history of success that draws quality people.

"Plus, we've got the most passionate people and biggest sports enthusiasts around. Oh, and the mountain landscape surrounding the city," he says with a sigh, "it's all so beautiful. Lake Washington and the Puget Sound are right here. Mount Rainier is a beautiful scenic view. I love it. The outdoors is the best."

"Mountains are so inspiring," I say.

"Oh, you've gotta see 'em out here then," Jason eagerly suggests.

"Wow. I appreciate you sharing that. Hopefully, we can be on the same team and work together sometime," I say.

"For sure. Good luck with your interview," he says.

"Thanks, Jason. Have a good day," I say, and end the call.

Really nice people out there in Washington, I think and begin typing a short introductory email.

Good morning, Grant,

My name is Joel Edmonds, and currently I am a store manager at Hank and Harry's Hardware in Des Moines, Iowa. I'm excited for the opportunity to continue growing market share and progress in my career with Hank and Harry's as your sales representative, opening the store in Seattle-Northlake. I believe my career with Hank and Harry's as a store manager in Des Moines brings a lot of valuable experience, and I look forward to discussing the opportunity with you.

I appreciate your consideration to be part of a new team and look forward to speaking with you in the future. Have a great day.

Regards,

Joel Edmonds

✱✱✱

The following weekend, it's nice outside and the backyard barbecue is back on. The blue sky on a spring day inspires me to find any excuse to go out and enjoy it. The sun's warmth on my skin with the cool breeze of early April has a subtle delight. Why not have a backyard barbecue?

As I pull up, I see Bobby Kozak, one of my best friends from college, lifting one of his kids out of their car seat. Today is also day three of The Personal Development Podcast Challenge, and the challenge was a demonstration activity: implementing new learning into action. I'm ready to put my new cognizance into practice. I notice Bobby's wife, Tiffany, waving as I park behind them.

"Hey guys," I say as I get out of the car. "What's going on? Hey, Alice," I say and wave to their three-year-old.

"Eddie! What's going on, man?" Bobby says. We do a handshake and hug. "It's been a minute."

"Yeah, it has. I'm excited to finally not be working and get some time out in the sunshine."

"Right? It's beautiful out today," Tiffany says, coming around the car with a baby carrier. She sets down the baby and hugs me. "It's good to see you. How are you holding up?"

"I'm pretty good. I've been working with a life coach for the last month, and things are starting to turn around at the store," I share.

"Yeah?" Bobby asks. "That's good to hear, man. Sorry I haven't reached out much since you got divorced. The new baby has been a bit of a handful."

"It's all good. Coach Thomas has been very supportive to talk to since I moved out of Evan and Mel's guest room. It's been quite a journey the last few months," I continue as we walk toward the backyard.

As we round the corner, I see Evan already has his cornhole bag toss game set up, and another friend, Gabe, is already here with his wife and kids. His dog and Evan's are wrestling around in the yard, tossing bags around.

"Hey! All right, everyone's here," Evan exclaims as we round the corner and make our way up the stairs to his back porch facing a shared community pond.

"I'm so excited you're all here," Mel begins, barely containing her enthusiasm. "We're having a baby!"

"Hey, congrats!" Gabe says, raising his beer.

"Wow, yeah! Congratulations," I say.

Tiffany hugs Mel, and so does Gabe's wife, Amber, who begins talking about her pregnancy experience.

Bobby cracks a beer. "Good job, buddy!" he jokes, raising his drink. "Welcome to sleepless nights and diaper duty. How do you feel?"

"I'm good. Excited," Evan says, taking a sip of his mixed drink from a large, forty-ounce cup.

I sit down at the patio table with them and grab an IPA from the cooler, opening it with the bottle opener on my keychain.

"That's why we wanted everyone to come over for a BBQ, to celebrate and share the news," Evan continues.

"This is great news," I say. "And speaking of news, I may not be in Des Moines when the baby is born," I share and take a sip of beer.

"What do you mean?" Gabe asks.

"Well, my assistant manager quit a couple of weeks ago, and I've been working with a life coach addressing the divorce and working in the store. It's been very supportive in figuring out where I want to go next. I'm considering relocating and applied for a position in Seattle," I share with everyone.

"I even sent the sales manager an email introducing myself and saying, 'Hey, I'm your next sales rep. I'm looking forward to meeting you,'" I continue.

"Did you say that?" Bobby asks in surprise.

"Something like that," I respond.

"Wow, good for you," Gabe says.

"Seattle?" Evan asks. "When did you start considering living out there?"

"Coach Thomas and I talked about stretching my comfort zone, and I got to thinking that Hank and Harry's has locations everywhere. I feel stuck on the South Side, and rep territories don't open up often in this district. It's all pretty recent," I explain.

"I couldn't do that. I love it here in Iowa," Bobby chimes in.

"Yeah, I love the small city Des Moines vibe too," I say in agreement. "It's great, but I don't ever see you all very much. I went out with a girl, Vanessa, a couple weeks ago. I don't know," I say, shaking my head. "I don't want to play the games and start over in Des Moines. There's more I want to experience, and I think there's a lot of opportunity in Seattle."

"I hope it works out," Evan says, as he fumbles with the propane tank on his grill.

"Thanks. It's been three weeks since the divorce was finalized," I add.

"Wow!" Gabe says, sounding shocked that it's already been that long.

Mel and Tiffany start tossing the blue and red bean bags back and forth on the cornhole game in the backyard with the kids while Gabe and Evan's dogs continue running around everyone.

"You could move away from here?" Mel asks.

"Well, I'm not going to see you two as much now that you'll be on baby duty. As soon as Bobby and Tiffany had their first kid, they were in the house on call. I get it. You'll be busy taking care of your kid," I say.

"I want to figure out who I want to be in a new place," I continue. "I've put some thought into it, and I could move to Chicago or LA, but there is something about living in Seattle."

"It rains," Bobby says jokingly.

"Well, hopefully I'll have an interview with the sales manager for the territory in Seattle," I say.

"This is something new. Aren't you scared?" Mel asks.

"No, I'm not scared," I say. "I think it's time for me to go and start living the life I felt wasn't possible before. There are things that I hadn't asked myself before about relationships, and there are things Angela and I didn't talk about before we got married."

At that moment, I realize how I truly feel about leaving Iowa and moving to Seattle. "Wow," I say, in shock. "I haven't said that to anyone yet."

"Well, we'll miss you if you leave," Evan says.

"Thanks. I'll miss all of you too. I've been thinking about Angela, the divorce, and that we were both doing our best at the time. I felt this deep uncertainty when I had the wedding ring thrown at me, like I didn't know what I was doing. Seeing my destroyed bobblehead . . ." I say, letting out a deep sigh. "I have to let it go too. I was opening up to Vanessa, but then another guy shows up that she's also dating, and she breaks up with me the next day. At some point, enough is enough.

"I realize how much baggage I've carried from every relationship I've been in, feeling like I was not good enough or that I couldn't trust myself and what I wanted. I've been so afraid of feeling like a failure in relationships. I'm done with excuses for not living a life of integrity," I continue. "I'm choosing to do something different. And that includes a change of scenery."

Everyone is looking at me intently. Mel breaks the silence. "What have you been up to?"

"I told you, this life coach has been very supportive with processing my experience," I say.

"Well, all right," Evan says, as he fires up the grill. "Let's get some tunes going and have a party. We've got a lot to celebrate!"

"Yeah!" yells Bobby's three-year-old daughter, Alice. We all laugh.

I look up at the blue sky and take a deep breath. "This is a great day. I'm so glad we're all together," I say.

***

On Monday morning, I get a phone call from Grant Holzman in Seattle, and we have more of a conversation than I was anticipating about the position in Seattle.

"Good morning, Joel, how are you?" he begins.

"I'm well, thank you, Grant. How are you?" I respond and ask.

"I'm well, thanks for asking. Joel, you caught my attention. We were about to repost the position for more candidates, but I wanted to follow up with you first," Grant begins. "Tell me about your experience working in the store."

"I recently had a situation with an employee that negatively impacted the store. The DM stepped in to resolve the issue, and now, with new staff and patient training, we're rebounding from being backward 16 percent to only 4 percent. Things are trending, and training the staff is going well," I say. "In the end, I'm looking for something new. I want to stretch my comfort zone, and I consider a city like Seattle to be that new place of opportunity."

"Well, it's a new territory if you're up for it," says Grant, revealing his reason for the conversation.

"It sounds like an excellent opportunity," I respond without hesitation.

"What are you looking for from your career overall? Where do you see yourself in five years?" Grant asks.

"Five years?" I begin thinking aloud. "I'm somewhere close to water and I'm inspired. I'm contributing to something bigger than myself, and I'm involved in things in the community. For example, we have a Grab N Go Grocery store under remodel by one of our customers. That customer's rep out here is also like a mentor to me, and I enjoy working with him. We support each other and working together has contributed to the store's successful rebound this year. He's got my back regardless of what I'm struggling with."

I continue, "Even though I had customers leaving, I'm not giving up on this store, and some customers are returning already. I don't want to leave Hank and Harry's—I believe in Hank and Harry's Hardware and what we're doing here for our community. I think this opportunity in Seattle will allow me to build on the experience I bring to the table."

"What challenges do you anticipate in having a new territory?" Grant asks. "How will you get yourself to pick up the phone and make calls when you hear the word *no?* Are you going to continue to call on customers, even if they're rejecting you right to your face?"

"I've been on the phone calling customers since my assistant manager left, inviting them back into the store. I'm not afraid to pick up the phone. I'm more excited to pick up the phone and share the opportunity now than I had been before," I respond. "And the word *no* is not a personal rejection in sales."

"I can tell you want to be part of a vibrant environment," Grant says.

"I do. Supporting this territory is an excellent opportunity to share my experience in a highly respected district and thrive within your passionate community," I say.

"Well, thanks for taking this call, Joel. We'll be in touch with you about the position this week," Grant says.

This week? That's soon, I think.

"Thank you for the opportunity and for the call. Have a great day," I say.

"You too, Joel," Grant says, and hangs up.

That evening, I complete the day-four challenge question from The Personal Development Podcast Challenge. It's called the Intentional Observation Activity: noticing how I'm behaving and responding to my environment while continuing to put new, deliberate actions into practice consistently.

> Be an observer of yourself. How are you creating situations in your life?
>
> What can you do? Even better yet, what do you choose to do? This exercise is about exercising your choice toward action around areas in your life that move you toward the vision you have created for your ideal life. If money was no issue and everything was safe and legal, write everything you can think of that you want to have, do, or be in your ideal town, city, or location—anywhere in the world. Expand your thinking here—and think big.
>
> Write down everything you can think of as a possibility, whether you currently see it as realistic or not, and put it on the list to do, be, have, accomplish, experience . . . you name it. This is the first step in designing your future possibility.

I click on the Begin Exercise icon on the bottom right of the screen after the video, and the next page loads.

Question 1: Who are you going to be? If your ideal version of yourself was walking down the street, what would you see? What would you be doing? How would you be any different than where you currently see yourself?

I take a moment to reflect before writing:

- *I'm confident in myself and the decisions I make. They're grounded in my values and reflect my best intentions.*

- *I'm open to giving and receiving love in an exclusive relationship.*

- *I'm loving the awe-inspiring views and scenery of the Pacific Northwest.*

- *I'm sympathetic and empathetic when I need to understand differing opinions and perspectives.*

- *I'm mindful of my decisions and how they affect others.*

- *I'm purposeful with my goal setting as I direct my life's path forward to the next step in my journey.*

- *I'm successful in my sales territory, hitting or exceeding sales goals.*

Question 2: What do you want to do? I begin typing again.

- *Ask a girl out, without any drama*

- *Purchase NHL season tickets*

- *Find a charity I want to volunteer for*

- *Live in a safe area where I can run on the trails and walk Presley*

- *Go for a hike*

- *Visit mountain ranges for a weekend getaway*
- *Learn to ski*
- *Make more than $100K in salary*
- *Run consistently outside when it's above freezing*
- *Spend time with people I want to spend time with who are inspiring and engaged with a values-driven purpose*
- *Complete The Personal Development Podcast Four-Day Challenge*

Question 3: If money was no issue, what would you have?

- *No debt*
- *Season tickets for hockey*
- *Monthlong vacations*
- *Freedom: time and resources to do what I want*
- *I'd be living the dream*

Question 4: How do you feel about your life now and about your future?

Everywhere has something to offer—something great to see, do, or experience and something that can be better. I'm satisfied with my life and the experiences I've had living in Iowa. It's time for me to do something different. Trusting myself and my desires will position me for my best opportunity to live a fulfilling life. I'm willing to do the work to get something new, and I want to keep taking the next step. One step forward is better than doing nothing. It's an exciting thought that the culmination of my actions in Iowa will result in a big step forward in Seattle. I will be in my passion and purpose and be open to giving and receiving love in Seattle.

***

On Wednesday afternoon, I get the call from Grant in Seattle that I've been waiting for. I answer, "Hank and Harry's Hardware. This is Joel speaking. How can I help you?"

"Hey, good afternoon, Joel. It's Grant Holzman in Seattle. How are you?" I hear him say cheerfully through the phone.

"I'm well, Grant. How are you?" I ask in response.

"I'm well, Joel. Do you have a moment?" Grant asks.

My heart sinks, and I walk from behind the storefront counter to the office to sit down.

"Yeah, I do. What's up?" I ask, beginning to sweat.

"Well, I wanted to be the first to reach out and thank you again for applying for the new Sales Rep Seattle-Northlake position. As I mentioned, we considered reposting the position to include more candidates. Still, after speaking with you on Monday, we decided that we'd like to offer you the position in Seattle and bring you on board with the Cascades District," Grant begins.

"Are you serious?" I say, almost jumping out of my chair.

"Joel, we love your passion for working with your staff and the community," he begins. "We're excited for you to bring that perseverance and enthusiasm to the new Seattle-Northlake position as you build your customer base."

"Oh, thank you so much, Grant. I accept!" I say, putting one of my arms in the air and fist-pumping.

"Awesome. So, to get the process started, there's some paperwork to fill out, but once we get that done, the relocation package will kick in, and we'll take care of getting you out here. It'll be about three days for your background check to clear, and we'd expect you to start here the Monday following that. So, you'd be looking at a week, maybe ten days before you'd start here," Grant says.

"Wow, that's soon!" I say, surprised at the turnaround time.

"It sure is, Joel. We at the district office are all super excited to bring you here. We're growing, and the new store will be lucky to have you and your drive. Keep an eye out for an email from our district coordinator in the next twelve to twenty-four hours," Grant instructs.

"I will. Thank you for the opportunity. I look forward to getting out there and getting started," I say. "Have a great rest of your day."

"You too, Joel. I'll be in touch. Congratulations again," Grant says before hanging up.

I'm so excited to be getting out of here that I call John immediately, but he doesn't answer, sending the call to voicemail. I hang up and sit down to send him an email.

> *Good afternoon, John,*
>
> *I wanted to give you a heads-up that I interviewed for a position in Seattle and just received an offer for a sales rep position out there. I've accepted the offer, and I'll be leaving in about a week to ten days for Seattle, once my background paperwork is processed. I called to share the news with you but got your voicemail.*
>
> *Have a good day.*

Joel

I head outside to the employee parking lot and get in my car for privacy. I begin yelling, "Wooooo!" at the top of my lungs and clapping my hands in celebration with no one around.

I head back inside to the office and notice that I've already received an email response from John.

Joel,

With the store having no assistant manager, we need you there until we can get someone placed. That's how it's done. There needs to be a manager in the store. Once we get help in the store, then you report to your next position.

John

My heart sinks immediately and I begin to feel heat rising from my stomach and spreading throughout my body in frustration.

"Are you serious?" I yell out loud and slam my hands on my desk. "There's no way I'm waiting and hoping for you to do your job," I shout at no one in the office. I click on the Reply tab and begin typing.

John,

I'm not asking you when I can leave. I'm telling you that I'm going. I called you directly to speak about this. If you have an issue with the start date, I will refer you to my new manager out in Seattle. I appreciate your support with removing Kim and the toxic presence in the store here on the South Side, but it's time for my new opportunity in a new place.

Joel

I click Send and close the email. I have very little desire to do much now, and I'm chomping at the bit to see the relocation options. *Three days from my background check clearing and I'll be on my way,* I think to myself.

When I get home after work, I grab my journal and begin writing.

> *Last page of this journal, and a new chapter of my life is about to begin. I'm about to move to Seattle, so why not begin with a new journal? It's all going to be different. That is good. This is what I'm going for and what I want. Working with Coach Thomas the last few months and completing the Personal Development Podcast challenge exercises makes me feel like I'm beginning a new phase of something special in my life.*
>
> *John telling me that I have to stay in the store is ridiculous. Where do I draw the line? His expectations are the same stressful demands where I sacrifice my physical and mental health in the store, and it's not worth it. I am here now and not yet where I am going. I don't expect it to be easy, but I also don't want to live and work frustrated like this. Keep breathing, Joel. Remember, you're making steps forward. Remember that you're passionate about helping people and that what you want matters.*

CHAPTER 14

The Conversation I Hoped to Avoid

When I get to the store the next morning, just as I suspected, there is another email from John.

Joel,

Call me at the district office.

John

"Ugh. I want out of the store now. I don't want to fight about what I want here," I say and roll my eyes.

I look at the clock, and it's six thirty. The last few months have been a draw on my will, and now is an opportunity to say that enough is enough. I grab some paper from the fax machine and begin to write.

> *I've been through challenges with Angela when I wasn't happy, and now in the store, it's starting to make me feel miserable. I'm done fighting and resisting what's happening here. I've done everything I can to succeed, and my options are to be in the store until they find a replacement or quit. How can I support Wyatt and Roselynn while I'm still here? How can I get ahead of George's next order since I'll be leaving in two weeks?*

I get up from my desk, heading to the break room to shake off my frustration and start making the morning pot of coffee.

Can I make these last few weeks so enjoyable that I appreciate this as an opportunity? I think to myself. "What can I do to shift my focus to what I do want?" I ask out loud.

As I contemplate that sentence, I notice the headlights from George's truck pull up in front of the store. I sigh and continue my morning routine to open the store.

When I unlock the front door, George gets out of his truck and heads into the store.

"Good morning, George. What's going on?" I ask. "How are things at the Grab N Go?"

"Hey, Joel! We're cruising right along and getting to the thick of it now," he says with a grin. "The guys need more drywall tape and a few other supplies, so I figured I'd get in early to get 'em started."

"Well, I'm glad you're here. I was thinking about you and getting ahead on your orders. I might be leaving the store in a few weeks," I say.

"Are you quitting too?" George asks.

"No, I applied for a sales rep position in Seattle and am working out the details about when I can go," I say.

"Oh yeah? Congratulations, man. I was going to ask you about that," he says with enthusiasm.

"You were?" I say, surprised by his response.

"Yeah. Junior said he was watching a video of you somewhere, and you were saying that you applied or were talking about feeling stuck and looking for help," he begins.

"How did he hear that?" I ask, confused. My mind begins to race, wondering where he could've seen a video of me, and then I remember: The Personal Development Podcast Four-Day Challenge exercises.

"Is Junior doing a podcast development challenge?" I ask, recognizing the connection.

"He's listening to all sorts of podcasts on jobs and talks about random challenges all the time," George says. "The renovation and remodeling industry in Des Moines is tight, Joel, and you've been instrumental in supporting Smart Renovations in getting to the next level in our business. What you're willing to go through to help us with this job and ensure that we have the material needed on time to start the most critical renovation for this company on the right foot means a lot."

He continues, "I've been on my own in business for over a decade now, and I've noticed a few things about this company when managers start to burn out. I don't want Hank and Harry's to lose a good man who's pouring his heart into this store and genuinely cares about his employees and customers. They've got to support you in having what's important to you too. That's only fair."

"Thank you for that, George. I wonder if it would help if John knew that," I say. "He's adamant that I stay here until he finds my replacement."

"If he doesn't know, I'd be happy to tell him that you work your ass off to support me and my business. As much as I hate to see you go, he's not doing you any service making you stay here," George says.

"You don't have to do that," I say.

"No, man, it's not right that they're forcing you to stay in the store," he continues in my defense.

I shrug my shoulders as the store's phone starts to ring. "Excuse me, George, I have to take this call. I appreciate your support and willingness to advocate for me," I say, heading toward the counter to grab a cordless phone. I answer as Roselynn walks in the employee entrance to begin her shift.

"Hank and Harry's, this is Joel. How can I help you?" I say.

"Good morning, Joel, it's John at the district office," I hear on the other end. "Do you have a moment?"

My heart sinks, and I don't want to be on this call yet. I take a deep breath and clear my throat, noticing the fear.

"Sure. Roselynn just walked in, and I was talking to George Martin about his grocery store renovation to prepare for what's coming next. What's up?" I ask, walking into the back warehouse, leaving Roselynn to finish up with George.

"Yeah, that's why I'm calling. I apologize if my email seemed short yesterday. I just wanted to discuss why it's not so simple for you to leave the store and move to Seattle," he says, maintaining his position.

"OK," I say, skeptical of what I will hear.

"Listen, we won't have someone hired in three days, regardless of what Grant said in Seattle. It's not possible to post a position, interview, and run all the necessary background checks to hire someone in three days for this. I understand you are excited about it, but we can't just have you disappear in this particular circumstance. The store is not going to have a manager or an assistant manager. We need you here," John begins.

"Have you spoken to Grant about this?" I ask.

"I've got a call out to him too," John responds.

"It'll be a couple of weeks at the soonest, but we can get the process started and completed. We're already looking for an assistant manager, but I don't anticipate the same challenge of people not wanting to accept a manager position in the store," he asserts.

"It doesn't make sense," I say, shaking my head. "I don't want to keep begging for help, John. I do what you asked me to. I do what I need to do to fulfill my store responsibilities. I ask for help when I need it, and now I'm stuck here?" I ask in disbelief.

"Listen, Joel. Just pause for a minute and take a breath. This process is going to take time. Without knowing the situation in the store to backfill your position, it's impossible for Grant to know entirely what your situation is, and he may be willing to accommodate us. You've still got the offer, so don't panic," John says.

I was beginning to panic, realizing how much I wanted to get out of this damned store.

"John, I've voiced my frustration with you before, and it's been a slow process to see any changes in the store here. I'm getting to my breaking point," I say, holding back tears of frustration.

"It will be more like at least two weeks, only four to seven days longer than what Grant initially suggested. What's another four days?" he says dismissively.

"John, I mean, what can I do?" I say, shrugging my shoulders. I sit in my chair and start massaging my head with my free hand. "These are twelve-hour days, and it's been a challenging year with the divorce and dealing with Kim. Every day it's something. I keep getting up and trying my best, so I'll continue to do what I can, John."

"Thank you, Joel. Hank and Harry's, especially your part-timers and customers, will appreciate that you have been here for as long as you were in this position," he says, trying to reassure me.

"Sure thing, John. I'll talk to you later," I say, eager to end the call.

"OK, have a good day, Joel."

"You too," I say and hang up, immediately exhaling with a loud sigh.

I walk out of the office and back up front.

"Good morning, Joel," Roselynn says. "How are you?"

"It's one of those days," I say, rubbing my hand over my neck.

"Well, there's another call for you. Grant Holzman is on hold," she says.

"From Seattle?" I ask and shoot back into a panic, pulling the cordless phone out of my pocket.

Roselynn shakes her head in front of her shoulders, unsure. "He hasn't been long," she says.

"OK, thanks, Roselynn," I say and pick up the line.

"This is Joel," I say, walking toward the warehouse loading dock.

"Hey, Joel, it's Grant out in Seattle. How are you doing today?"

"Hey, sorry for the delay. I was on the other line with John," I begin. "It sounds like I am still here for at least two weeks, so he can find a replacement for me because there's no assistant manager in the store. I asked him to reach out to you to coordinate my transition."

"Yeah, I spoke with John. I understand the store situation and the urgency a little bit better, and this situation happens. It's common for the transfer to take some time. It can take about a week, but the two-week time frame is more realistic. The store does need you, by the sound of your district manager. According to him, there's you and two part-time employees, and two of them are new hires."

I'm still stuck in the store, I think, and the negative thought cycle begins again. *I didn't have the help I needed when I asked for it. I have an opportunity to leave and now I can't because there's no help in the store. I can't win.*

"Thanks, Grant," I say, taking a deep breath. "If this is a more realistic expectation, I will focus on making the next two weeks enjoyable and supportive for my staff and customers. I can continue the momentum we're building in the store here. Thank you for your reassurance," I say, accepting the news.

"You know what they say: the night is always darkest before dawn. Your sunrise is coming, Joel. Before you know it, you'll be on the West Coast," Grant says.

"Thanks, Grant. I hadn't thought of it that way," I admit.

After we end our call, I schedule a last-minute call with Coach Thomas for later this evening to discuss the curve ball regarding my delay in transferring to Seattle.

When I arrive home that evening, it's still an hour before twilight. Coach Thomas made an exception for the late call tonight at eight o'clock.

"Good evening, Coach Thomas. How are you?" I ask.

"I'm well, Joel. How are you?" he asks.

"Well, I know we only have two calls left." I pause and take a breath. "A transfer I applied for in Seattle has been delayed. I want to approach this situation differently than how I typically react and not stress out. While I'm still in Des Moines, I'm trying to see the bright side of things, and I thought I could use your support."

"Wow. Congrats, Joel. That is quite a step forward. So, what's going on?" Coach Thomas asks.

"Well, I've received an offer, but I'm not sure when I can go. I was on the phone with my district manager this morning, and he told me I have to stay in the store because they have no assistant manager, and it will take a while to find a replacement for both positions.

"It doesn't make sense that I must stay and continue to be subject to the very thing that makes me want to get out of here. I'm certain I don't want to be a manager in the store anymore. As much as I try to explain, conversations with John leave me more stressed than before. As much as I try to pay attention to something different and focus on something different or serve someone from a place of compassion and supporting what's important to them, I feel like I'm not getting any satisfaction from my effort. Is there something I can do to help manage my stress and frustration with this situation?"

"You're really focused on getting out of the store. What does it mean for you to get out of there so quickly?" Coach Thomas asks.

"Now, without an assistant manager, I'm still stuck here, and I don't want to feel this way. I don't like coming to work, being stressed every day, and having situations like the one with Kim play out," I say.

"What if you reframed the context, and what you call a *problem* became an *opportunity*? What opportunities could you see from the perspective of creating the environment you do want?" Coach Thomas asks.

"Well," I say, then pause, getting lost in thought. "I don't know."

"This mindset of needing to get out of here and that you need something else is tiring. If you trust the process to play out, how can you support this store's transition and take action around creating your vision for what you want? What do you think that would do for your energy?"

"I'd feel more energized," I respond. "I picture my vision demonstrating my commitment to action and expansion. My life will be full of meaningful experiences moving forward, and looking back, I can see how these experiences are in service of making progress moving forward," I say, shifting in my chair.

"How are you being with that in action?" Coach Thomas asks.

"I'm coming up with a plan for what I want and dealing with what's in the way when something comes up. It might not make it easier or make it less stressful, but over time I could see the changes," I say in response.

"Taking action and not seeing results immediately could be tricky, but you know what you want. And that seems to keep inspiring you to take new action," Coach Thomas says. "Continue engaging and talking about the things you're struggling with or that frustrate you. That's where the change happens. That's where the magic is."

✳ ✳ ✳

Two weeks later, they officially announce my replacement. Before I leave, I spend a few hours training the new manager, and then I introduce them to George and a couple of other key customers.

CHAPTER 15

The Life Worth Living

Yes, Seattle, this is happening!" It's Sunday night, and I'm pretty excited as I make my way into the city for the first time. Pulling into the parking garage of the hotel, I park my car and walk into the lobby.

I'm greeted at the front desk by a well-dressed woman in a green button-down shirt branded with an Emerald City Suites logo. She hangs up the phone as I approach the counter.

"Good evening. Welcome to Emerald City Suites. Do you have a reservation?" she says.

"Hi. Yes, I do. I'm just getting into town from Des Moines, Iowa." I hand the front desk agent my ID.

"Oh, wow. Welcome to Seattle," she says and begins typing.

"What brings you out this way?" she asks, sliding my ID back to me across the counter.

"I'm relocating out here. Tomorrow's my first day, and I'm exhausted," I say. I look around the hotel, taking in the breakfast bar to my right and the lounge areas behind me, with the evening cable news report on the TVs.

"Well, Mr. Edmonds, your room is on the fifth floor, right on the corner. You're all set," the attendant says, handing me my room keys. "The elevator is right over there," she says pointing and highlighting a small map that contains my room key.

"Thank you," I say, grabbing the keys. I head out to get Presley from the car and begin the fun process of unloading a packed car after a twenty-seven-hour trip.

The front desk attendant wasn't kidding about the room being right on the corner. I'm overlooking an intersection here on Capitol Hill.

"This place is enormous, Pres, huh?" I say, letting her off her leash in our temporary new home. Presley begins running around the room, sniffing her new surroundings.

I go for a walk up Pike Street to Capitol Hill, eager to explore a little bit of the neighborhood. There's a burger place, a sushi place, and coffee shops everywhere. There are more people in a Star City Coffeehouse at seven o'clock in the evening than I would've ever expected to see.

I pop into Capitol Burgers and order a sandwich and fries to go. "A Staple of the City and Business Since 1951" reads a sign as I enter.

Eating my meal in the hotel room, I spend a few hours online looking at apartments and watching people from the corner window. The vibe and the people walking around the neighborhood seem like the energy I've been looking for. I'm excited to explore the city and see what it offers. I open my journal and begin to write.

> *Life doesn't always happen according to your plans or your timeline. I don't want it to be the first thing I do, but I do want to date someone at some point.*

I look out the window, excited that this is the city where it will happen.

The following day, I drive through the mountains for the second time ever, heading toward the district office in Snoqualmie, and it's quite an experience. No more days of commuting from Des Moines to Cedar Rapids and trying to stay awake driving across miles of farmland. Now I'm wide-awake, weaving through mountains. There's still snow in a few places here in April, which I guess is standard in the Pacific Northwest. It would be in the sixties in Des Moines now.

Arriving at the office, I walk in, ready to meet Grant for the first time. "Good morning," the office administrator says, smiling as I enter.

"It's my first day on the job here. I just relocated to the district," I say.

"Ah, Grant said he had a new hire coming in today. I'm Bridget, the district's office manager. I'll let Grant know you're here."

Today is day one of being a sales rep.

"Hey, Joel, welcome." Grant walks out of his office, not far from where I'm standing. We shake hands.

"How are you doing, Grant?" I ask with a big smile.

"Good. Nice to finally meet you in person. How was the trip in?" he says with a grin of his own.

"It was a long trip, but I had a lot of coffee. Driving to the district office is no joke either," I say. "It took an hour to go less than thirty miles."

"Yeah, I suggest that you add at least thirty minutes to every trip, knowing the traffic will only worsen," Grant says. "You'll get used to it." He waves me into his office.

Behind Grant's desk are multiple trophies and plaques displaying his achievements. We each sit down at his desk.

"So, this is a new sales territory," he begins, getting comfortable in his chair.

I nod.

"It's going to take some creativity to get this thing off the ground. I was excited about what you were able to accomplish in Des Moines, given your circumstances, and the experience you bring to this district," he continues.

"Thank you. I love working for the company," I respond.

"We have a large client and customer database that we can scrub for local small businesses and potential contractors and customers in the area who have shopped at Hank and Harry's before. These customers are potential Pro Account customers that we can convert to our preferred program. Your responsibility is to reach out to all the leads we've identified and convert them into loyal buying customers." He slides a thick folder of potential customers across his desk to me.

Wonderful, I think to myself. *Just call everybody on the list. It's that simple.* I flip through the first couple pages, each which has at least a dozen names, phone numbers, and addresses printed.

"So, I'll be calling everyone on this list," I repeat. A new sense of overwhelming anxiety emerges in my chest. "I have to call all these people. I can do that."

"Take a breath, Joel," Grant says. "We don't have your company phone set up just yet, but I would imagine it's coming within the next week. In the meantime, the store is coming together in

Northlake. Michelle and Zach are putting it together, and they could use a hand. It could be an excellent opportunity to get to know everyone."

"Yeah. I don't want to come in like I know everything, though. I want to help the store, too," I reply.

"Wonderful. Do you have any questions for me? Have you driven around the city much yet?" Grant asks.

"No, I didn't get in until last night and haven't had a chance to get around yet. Maybe I can drive around the city, talk to some of the other stores, and get to know some of my coworkers?"

"Yeah, spending some time at the store and visiting different stores in the area and introducing yourself would be a great way to get yourself out into the market. The city itself doesn't cover a lot of area like Chicago or Houston, but still, it can be confusing to make your way through the neighborhoods around here. I think it's unique how there's water on two sides of the city," he says, leaning back in his chair and glancing out the window. "I love the mountains as a backdrop with the lakes out here."

"It's beautiful here. I'm just not used to driving through those mountains yet," I admit.

"What did you think of driving over the floating bridge on I-90 on the way in?" Grant says with a smile and a nod.

"Yeah, that was unexpected coming in, but I'm sure I'll get used to it," I say, repeating his assertion from earlier.

"This year, you have to sell $1 million in your territory for things to pay off for Hank and Harry's. Some of it will transfer with a few customers we'll move to you to get you started. But it'll be up to you to get this off the ground. I'm sure you can get creative to find ways to drive business into the store."

"Yeah. Yeah, I can do that," I say with some nervousness. "This is part of the job."

"This is no big deal, Joel. Just do what you can," he says calmly. "Since we don't have your work phone yet, and some of the tools we need for you are still on the way, you could support the store while it's being put together. They have some shelving and freight coming in this week.

"Also, get something to take with you — cookies or sports drinks are always appreciated," Grant suggests. "We can discuss reimbursement and all that as things get going."

"Thanks. I'll do that," I say, accepting the suggestion.

"When you get your phone in the next week, start calling this list. We put a lot into getting this prospect list, so add the leads and prospective customers to your day planner."

"I don't have one of those yet," I say, reminding Grant I'm still on day one.

He pulls on a box behind his desk, and after shuffling around a bit, hands me a brown leather binder with an embroidered Hank and Harry's logo and the saying *Be the Best* printed on it.

"Wow, thank you, Grant," I say, staring at my gift.

"Don't worry about it," he responds casually.

After leaving the district office, I stop by potential apartments before heading over to the hotel to change into gym clothes to help put the store together. We'll be sweating in the store, so I decide to take Grant's advice and bring some beverages and snacks. Deep down, I want to break the ice, and I hope to set a positive tone for the entire week. We open in two weeks, so it's time for the rubber to hit the road.

When I pull into the store parking lot, it appears that everything has shown up at the store today: shakers, display shelves, registers, lighting, all being unloaded from a semitruck out front. "Tomorrow, the first load of three will show up to stock the store for the first time," I hear from the back of the truck as I walk toward the store's entrance.

"Good morning, all. I'm Joel Edmonds, the supporting sales rep for this store," I announce through the commotion.

"Hey, Joel. Nice to meet you. I'm Michelle Campos, the store manager," says the familiar voice from the truck. We shake hands.

"Good morning, I'm Zach Mazurek, assistant manager," I hear from inside the store's doorway. We also greet each other and shake hands.

"Nice to meet you. How are things going?" I ask.

"Oh, you know, just trying to figure out where to put all these boxes so we can get organized and put the shelving units together," Michelle says, placing her hands on her hips and looking around the store as we walk in.

"I apologize for not getting out here last week," I begin. "I'm coming from a challenging situation, and my district manager literally wouldn't let me leave. Now I feel like I'm late for the store opening."

"Are you here to help?" Zach asks.

"Yeah. I changed quickly at the hotel and headed over after my meeting at the district office this morning. I thought it'd be a good opportunity to see the store and meet everyone. I bought drinks and snacks," I say, holding up two grocery bags of sports water and energy drinks and bags of cookies and chips.

"Awesome," Zach says.

"Yeah, thanks for that. We really appreciate it. We've been working around the renovation team this last week. They just painted the walls a couple days ago," Michelle says, pointing around the storefront.

"Wow, it does smell like fresh paint in here," I say. "So how long have you all been here?"

"I've been on board for three years," says Zach.

"I'm six years with H&H. This is my first position as a store manager," says Michelle. "How about you?"

"Me? I'm seven years in," I say.

"What brings you to Seattle?"

"Well, I was looking for an opportunity for a fresh start. I'm coming from Des Moines. I'm recently divorced, and I had a pretty rough time in my store with an assistant manager. I was turning things around, and then I decided a change of scenery would be best for me. Plus, all my best friends have kids, so they're pretty busy, and I figured, why not?" I explain. "After doing a little research, I realized how much I love the region here, with all the trees and the mountains nearby—plus volcanoes! It's beautiful."

"I agree," says Zach. "I transferred here from Missouri."

"We'll need to earn each dollar that comes through this store. It will be hard. One step at a time. No mountain is climbed in a day," Michelle says.

"Let's face it. No one will ever be 100 percent prepared," I add. "I've learned that we can help customers realize how partnering with us can keep them competitive in the home remodeling and maintenance markets. We can contribute to the growth and financial success of the community by having more to offer."

As our conversation picks up, we find ourselves working together, and there's even a bit of laughter. I like this group, and I think I'll be just fine here in Seattle.

***

The tools I need begin arriving the following Monday. Selling brochures, a training binder, and all the instructions for what actions I should be taking when starting as a new Hank and Harry's sales representative. I'm spending the day with Grant today beginning at ten, and I'll either start my calls at the store or drive around with Grant to meet new customers.

As Grant walks into the store, he greets everyone. "Good morning, Michelle," he says, walking up and shaking her hand. "Good morning, Joel. Are you ready for our ride together today?" he asks.

"Good morning, Grant," I say. "I'm ready, I guess."

He notices the stores phone lines are just now being set up in the office. "You haven't been calling customers from here?" he asks.

"No, the phone company had a delay last week, and we're just getting the phones set up," Michelle says from inside the office.

"You could've gone to another store and made some calls, I guess," Grant suggests.

"I had no idea I could do that. The new store phone is sitting on the floor, and Michelle and Zach don't even have desks in their office until tomorrow. They've been sitting on paint buckets."

"Well, it should be set up soon. What have you been up to?" Grant asks.

"Well, I still don't have business cards, a phone, or email. So I found a place to live and moved my stuff," I say.

"Have you been calling anyone from your personal phone?" Grant asks.

"Not from my personal phone. I've seen customers get hold of the manager's number and call them at all hours during the week and flood them with calls on the weekends," I respond.

He hands me a white box. "Your phone has arrived. You can call IT for support if you need help setting it up. You can officially start calling customers," Grant says, smiling.

"Awesome!" The phone turns right on, everything is streamlined, and I'm working within ten minutes.

"So, what do you think of the prospect list?" Grant asks.

"It's thirty-five pages deep, with thirteen potential customers per page," I say, shrugging my shoulders. "I imagine some numbers are incorrect, but it's approximately 455 opportunities. I'll reach out to every prospect on the territories list now that I have the phone. I've also been driving around, trying to get familiar with the area. These hills are really steep in some places."

Michelle gives me some of her cards. "Why not try knocking on some doors, too, and hand these out," she suggests.

I take the cards from her and look at Grant.

"Let's go for a ride," Grant says. "You can tell me more about what you have been up to." We get in the car and head over to Rainier Beach, looking for one of the addresses on my prospect list.

"What number are you on?" Grant asks.

"Seven," I respond.

"Nice. Do you know where you're heading?" Grant asks.

"Not really, but I'm following the GPS on my phone to the address on this list," I say.

"If you don't see it, don't stop," Grant says.

We stop outside a property with the correct address, and the sign's name matches the lead sheet's name. We park the car out front and get out. I nervously approach the door and pull on the handle. The doors are locked, but there's a contact phone number on the handwritten sign that says *Sorry, we're temporarily closed.*

"You should give them a call," Grant suggests.

"Right now?" I ask.

"Sure, why not?" Grant says, and we walk back to the car and get in. I pull out my company phone and dial the number from the sign. The pressure is on, and I start to sweat.

"I call it a discovery call because a cold call has a negative undertone of failure. You're not calling to sell anything. You're building relationships and discovering who is a potential customer versus someone who sees no value in working with you," Grant explains as the phone rings. "Everyone has something you can connect value to. Build your territory by finding your customers' needs that we can fill and add to that value from the experience they get interacting with you or the new store that they can't get anywhere else. Every *no* leads to a *yes* eventually."

The phone rings and ends up going to voicemail. "Hey Jerry, this is Joel Edmonds with Hank and Harry's and Seattle's new Northlake store. Today I stopped by your shop to introduce myself as the new Hank and Harry's Hardware outside sales rep. I'm covering the city and want to discuss partnering with Hank and Harry's to satisfy your hardware and home remodeling needs. Give me a call back at (206) 513 . . ." I pause, say "8-2 . . ." and then I go silent and, in a panic, hang up. I look at Grant; he is staring at me. As I was talking, I realized that I have no idea what my phone number is. There is only silence in my car. I know it. We both know it. I'm not prepared.

I grab a pen, write my phone number on one of Michelle's cards, and say, "So that went well. Should I call him back?"

"Of course," Grant says. "Say your phone had trouble or something, then just leave the number."

I call back and play it off like the phone had an issue, and I had terrible reception. I'm going to make a mistake once in a while. We next visit a location that turns out to be a boarded-up house and eventually find the condominium a few blocks over. I notice a corkboard with the office number posted in an entryway, and Grant sends a text message to a group chat he has going to see if someone might be able to help us get in the door.

"If you come across something like this, you can text this group," Grant says, showing me his phone screen. "It's a group of other reps on your team. If you need support, have a question, or find something that will help the team, you can also share that. Let me add you to it now." He begins to type my name in the add member option on his smartphone.

"Is there anything else I can I do to get some support? I feel like I'm making all this up as I go," I say in embarrassment. "Is there anyone I can observe to see how things are done, to at least figure out how to get my feet under me?" I ask.

"We can schedule a rep observation, and you can shadow them for a day," Grant says, agreeing with my request.

"Yeah, that would help," I say.

"Let me make a couple of calls so I can set that up for you," Grant says, taking his cell phone and scrolling for a moment, and then makes a call.

"Hey, Anthony, it's Grant here. Hey, I got a new rep that we just brought in from Iowa, and I want to see if you have some availability this week to take a shadow with you for a day. When are you free?" he asks.

"Oh, OK, wonderful," he says. "Joel, are you free—oh, wait, of course you're free. You just got your phone, and the store isn't open."

"Yeah, I'll tell Joel to meet you on Thursday at eight o'clock at the store in Interbay. Have a great day, Anthony," Grant says, ending the conversation.

"That was Anthony Rivas. He has a $4 million territory, and he's been a rep for about eleven years. He's a great person to shadow. This guy is a bull and moves the sales needle," Grant explains.

***

Three days later, I walk into the Interbay store at eight o'clock. I see a guy that I assume is Anthony standing over the coffee machine, pouring himself a cup and mixing in creamer and sugar.

"Good morning. Are you Anthony?" I ask.

"Hey," he says with enthusiasm. "Yeah, good morning, you must be Joel. Anthony Rivas." He looks like the typical sales rep in his button-down shirt and khaki pants.

"Yes, Joel Edmonds," I reply. We shake hands.

"Welcome to Seattle. They're sure throwing you into the fire with the new territory, huh?" Anthony says.

"Yeah. I can tell you what's happening in a store, but being a rep is new to me. I've started calling the leads on this prospect list, and I don't know . . . some of the leads aren't very good so far. I'm visiting a lot of bad addresses and calling a lot of disconnected phone numbers. I feel like I'm wasting time," I say.

"How are you wasting it?" Anthony asks.

"No one is showing me how to do the job I'm trying to do," I respond.

"So? Make it up as you go," he says, shrugging his shoulders.

"I think Grant expects more activity in less time, and that's not how things are working out for me right now. I've driven around with Michelle, looking for some of these customers too. It was good to talk to her about what I'm dealing with, and it sounds like she's getting the same pressure," I say.

"The store is opening in just a week, right?" Anthony asks.

"The soft opening is next week," I say, nodding my head.

"Yeah, I've heard that we do things differently here than some other districts. We have a standard and expectation for performance that keeps communication open and supports a community feel. I think we all work well together because of it," Anthony says.

I follow Anthony into the back warehouse and the employee break room. The store looks exactly like my old store in Des Moines, but larger. The warehouse is bigger, too, and the loading dock can fit two semitrucks.

We walk past Maxwell, the store manager here in Interbay.

"Good morning, Max. This is Joel, a new rep out of Idaho that's shadowing me today," Anthony says, introducing me.

"I'm from Iowa actually. Joel Edmonds," I say and extend my hand.

"Maxwell Hanger. I'm the manager here. Welcome to the area. You gotta watch this guy," he jokes, slapping Anthony on the back and chuckling.

"Don't scare the man," Anthony jokes. He looks at me and says, "You're in good hands, my friend, I promise you that."

I smile. "Hey, at this point, I'll take all the help I can get. I have to get new accounts opened up, and I'm off to a slow start, according to Grant."

"Well, good luck today. Let me know if I can help out," Maxwell says again and heads back toward the storefront.

We walk into the break room and have a seat at one of the tables.

"So, tell me about what you've seen so far out here. We've got a nine o'clock appointment, but we've got some time before we need to head out."

"Not all of the accounts I'm calling on are prospects. Some are on other reps' territories already, so I'm wondering why they have two people in the same market calling on the same prospective customers?" I begin.

"You know, I've been a rep for eleven years, covering a $4 million territory. Going crazy is what they want. Just remember, the day starts with us, though. Start the store at 8:00 a.m.," Anthony advises.

"OK," I say, nodding my head.

As we start out, Anthony is checking his email while driving. Noticing my look, he smiles and says, "If you're moving at a decent pace and having time for everything or you find yourself just hanging out at stores and not ignoring lunch, you're not going to do well. If you're going crazy and have so much to do and feel like there's not enough hours in the day, you're doing it right. So, load up your time on your schedule out here."

That's not what I want. I want balance in my life between work and my personal life. "It was crazy in my previous store, and I was miserable," I say to Anthony. "That's why I left in the first place. I'm not here to lose myself for Hank and Harry's."

"Well, let's get started, and I'll show you how I go about my day," Anthony says, putting his phone down. "I'm regularly working bids and answering emails until 9:00 p.m."

"You work from 7:00 a.m. until 9:00 p.m.?" I ask, wide-eyed.

I think to myself, *This is my role model for the day, and it's his choice how he runs his territory. I don't have to be like him. Putting this level of effort into my territory may lead me to success, but I don't have to be the guy who answers his emails while driving.*

"Listen, you don't have to be the rep who puts work before everything else in life," Anthony says, noticing my response. "Life is sales and sacrifice. The money is good, and the sales are rolling in on my end."

"Listen, man. This is all you have to do," he says, waving his hands. "You gotta call all your leads, show up every day, and don't take the word *no* personally. It's no big deal. I wake up in the morning, head to the store first thing to check on what's going on, and see what they need before heading out to the territory. I'll bring some food for the car to snack on during the day, and I won't eat until I go home." Anthony explains.

"Really?" I ask, amazed by his dedication and his perspective of his role.

"Yeah. This way, I focus on creating momentum by seeing as many people as possible daily. Having grapes and almonds in the car is helpful," Anthony says, pointing to a large cooler in his backseat.

"Well, all right," I say. "Where are we heading?"

"We're heading to find a customer, Shasha's Shop. I set them up an account about a year ago, and I've called on them a few times but didn't get a response. People buy from those they know, like, and trust," Anthony says.

"Right now, nobody knows me," I say.

Anthony continues, "I figure, stop in about an hour after they open to build relationships and generate business opportunity. Every day can and will bring you challenges and also opportunities. It's up to you to figure out how to deal with them. Learn from every experience and then move on. Life will continue. I just continue to push through."

I get a text from Zach.

RE: A package was dropped off at store for you.

"Can we swing by the Northlake store? I just got a text from Zach, and I have a package to pick up. It must be more tools to get started in the territory. We can check out how the store is looking."

"Sure, we're not that far from it," Anthony says, and we make a quick detour.

As we pull in front of the store, the number of work trucks and vans have significantly decreased since my first day. "You can tell we're getting close to the opening," I say to Anthony. "They just painted the drywall a few days before I got here, and now the store is filling up."

I walk through the sliding glass door entry and see Michelle and Zach putting together a Backyard and Barbecue-themed display for the store's grand opening.

"What's up—showtime?" I say to Michelle.

"I wish I could say the same thing to you, but you aren't bringing in any new accounts," Michelle says unexpectedly.

"Damn, where'd that come from? We aren't even open yet," I respond in surprise.

"We're going to be open soon," she says with an attitude. "And we're not getting any preorders yet."

"Preorders? Who said anything about preorders?" I ask, looking at Anthony as if he would know what was going on.

"That's what we do out here before a store is open. We start lining up orders and getting customers signed up. We don't have any credit apps signed," Michelle says in a moment of frustration.

"I've barely even gotten my phone dialed in," I say. "I only came by because a package with training materials was just delivered to the store today."

She rolls her eyes and sighs.

"You OK?" Anthony asks, jumping into the conversation.

"Listen, I don't know what that is about. Do you have something to say?" I asked more directly.

"Yeah. You took this territory and moved out here. How do you not have people registered already?" Michelle continues.

"Before you get frustrated with me and say I'm not committed here, remember this is my first time opening a new store and starting a new sales territory, so it's new to me if this is part of your process. I've been here for less than two weeks," I say in my defense.

"This is part of the process we've got to do before the store opens," Michelle says.

"Good. I am making my way through my prospect list, but it's not turning up anything," I say.

"Well, keep calling, please," Michelle asks.

Anthony pulls out his phone, puts it up to his ear, and says, "Hello? Hold on a second, I can't hear you," and walks out the front doors.

"Michelle, we're on the same team here. I'd like to see how you'd do, driving around a new city without a company phone, calling disconnected phone numbers, and stopping at addresses that don't add up to what a prospect list says they're supposed to be," I say, revealing the results of my activity so far.

"I'm sorry, Joel, my DM is really pressuring me. He keeps asking me about how many applications we have coming in, and I keep telling him none. He's giving me a hard time," Michelle says.

"Really? Grant hasn't said anything to me about it. I am out here driving around trying to figure this out without having any training. That's why I'm with Anthony today. To see what the hell it is I'm supposed to be doing compared to what I've been doing. You can trust that I'm on it and will do what I said I'm going to do. Take a breath. You don't have to give me an attitude if something is up. We're all new at this, and the store isn't open yet. Even if I brought you fifteen applications today, you're not going to be able to sell them anything," I say.

"Don't take it personally, Joel. We all want this store to be successful," Zach says, trying to calm the mood.

"When times get tough, shit rolls downhill. I imagine they're feeling stress and heat at the top. We have to show something, but again the store isn't open, and we're at the beginning of the journey," I say.

I walk to the counter and see two packages with my name on them. I open the small package while Zach awkwardly continues his assembly of the BBQ display.

"Look at that," I say in fake surprise. "Now I have business cards for prospecting, with my name printed on them rather than those I was handing out with my name handwritten on them."

I open the larger box and it contains my company tablet and product demo kit.

"Well, this will make life a lot easier for all of us," I say, shuffling the items around the box and folding the box shut. "Well, I'll see you later. This is what I came by for," I say, motioning with the box as I move toward the front door.

"See ya, Joel," Zach says.

"Have a good weekend, Joel. We'll figure out the app thing," Michelle says.

"Right on. See you later," I say and walk outside toward Anthony's car. He's sitting inside with his tablet on his lap typing an email.

"Hey, Joel, how are things going?" he says with a smirk as I get in his car.

"Shitty," I respond.

"What happened in they're just now? I had to walk out," Anthony says.

"Michelle is stressed," I say.

"I feel like we're coming along. I've called between fifteen to twenty people each day since I got the phone two days ago, and

I've driven around the city looking for shops that don't match the addresses I've been given," I explain.

"Well, good for you, doing all that and making calls," Anthony says, putting his tablet away and starting his car. "They're building a good crew in there, but again, it takes time. Enjoy the process, Joel."

"As I said, Joel," Anthony continues, "focus on helping the store reach customers. Look for any customers from nearby stores falling through the cracks. They are opportunities. Help them to be successful and direct those customers to the stores. Connect those people."

"Thanks for that," I say.

"No problem," Anthony says.

Later that afternoon, we arrive back at the Interbay store, and Anthony parks next to my car.

"All right, it's been good showing you around for a few hours," Anthony begins. "I'm gonna go post up and send off a few quotes I've gotta get out before the end of the day."

"More work?" I ask.

"It never ends, my friend. I'll see you later," he says, extending his hand, and we shake.

"I'll see you. Thanks again for taking a few hours to show me around," I say.

"Keep your head up," he says as I get out.

When I get back to the apartment, I grab my journal and begin to write.

OK, well, this is a rough week. Everyone's getting pissed, and I forgot my phone number while leaving a voicemail. I need to get around some new people. Why not go to a meetup? I mean, tomorrow is Friday, and I'm in a new city by myself. I may have just moved into an apartment, but I can still do something enjoyable.

CHAPTER 16

Finding Possibility

I walk over to The Connect Lounge on 2nd Avenue and stand in line to enter. Looking around, I notice a large blackboard with the phrase *Put your phones away and connect.*

When it's my turn to approach the check-in table, I begin by saying, "I'm not sure if I'm in the right place. I'm here for the new-to-town meetup."

"Hey, welcome. You're in the right place," says the young man with a handlebar mustache sitting behind the registration table inside the door. "There's also a singles meetup here too."

"Really?" I ask.

"Yeah," he continues with a smile. "You never know who you'll meet at The Connect Lounge."

"I like it." I grab a name tag and make my way into the crowded lounge. The small bar's orange, black, and white color scheme complements the couch seating. There are a few booths, some tables and chairs, and an L-shaped bar. People are writing catchphrases on the chalkboard near the front window, adding to the colorful chalkboard art. One reads:

> *Thanks for being where we can come together and connect as ourselves.*

It's about ten minutes after the start time, and about forty or fifty people are already here socializing. I make my way toward the bar and notice a beautiful woman with long brown hair in a braid making her way toward a table near the bar, and she sits down. The group at the table is playing some kind of card game, but I can't tell what through the crowd. We catch each other's eyes for a moment, and she flashes a smile before rejoining her conversation. A shot of electricity shoots straight through me.

As I get to the bar to buy a drink, I look around the room, wanting to connect and wondering how to tell who is single and looking and, like me, is out looking for new friends and having a good time.

As I get my drink, I turn toward a conversation in progress with a group standing to my left, and I awkwardly wait for a break in the conversation.

"Hey, everyone, how are you all doing?" I begin. "I'm Joel."

"Hey, what's up? I'm Phillip," says a thirtysomething blond male with a fresh beard and wearing a red flannel shirt.

"Terrance," the youngest in the group says, extending his hand and introducing himself. "How are you doing?" he continues. He's dressed more like a typical Seattle hipster, in a black shirt with black pants and wearing a black beanie. His brown jacket is the centerpiece that brings the all-black outfit together.

"Hi, I'm Beth," says a woman at least ten years younger than me. She looks beautiful in her blue plaid jacket and skinny jeans. How she can stand in her white heels must've required practice. I guess she's part of the singles meetup based on her constant scan of the room and sudden interest.

"What brings you out tonight?" Phillip asks.

"I'm new in town. I just moved to town from Des Moines about a week and a half ago," I say.

"Yeah? What brings you here?" Terrance asks, jumping in.

"I wanted to set down roots somewhere new and there was a job opportunity. I'm looking for a fresh start," I respond.

"Excellent," says Terrance.

Phillip continues, "Yeah, I just moved here about a year ago, and Terrance moved here about eight months ago with his partner, Michelle. Is that right?"

"Nine months now, but yeah," Terrance says, raising his eyebrows.

"Have you been to the Pike Place Market yet?" Michelle asks, joining the conversation.

"No," I say. "I haven't done any exploring other than going to work and driving around the city."

"You should check it out," Phillip says. "It's pretty cool."

Terrance chimes in, "Yeah, it's a tourist hotspot. That's also where the original Star City Coffee location is."

"Yeah?" I say in surprise. "I forgot they were from Seattle. They're everywhere."

"You can get fresh fish and produce at Pike Place, which is good," Philip says.

"Really?" I say in surprise. "So it's not just shops to buy touristy stuff, but an actual market?"

"Yeah. I get there early because it gets pretty packed. There are lots of people who buy their groceries there. Check it out sometime."

Across the room someone begins to yell, "If you don't like Mike, stop coming to Mike's events!"

"Sounds like someone is pissed about Mike combining meetups again," Phillip jokes.

"I've been to a few of his events, which are usually pretty entertaining. There's always one person who's upset, though. They don't like constantly being hit on," Terrence says.

"You want to grab a drink?" Phillip asks.

"Sure," I respond. I finish my whiskey sour, and we head back to the bar.

The lounge is beginning to fill up now. The shortest line is behind us, next to the table with the brunette that caught my attention earlier.

Phillip and I make our way around the bar, toward where the brunette is sitting, and we stand in line.

"So, what's the deal with this Mike guy?" I ask. "Why are people freaking out about attending his meetups?"

"Well, I'm sure you can see there are a ton of people here now. Mike likes to randomly organize multiple group events at the same place so he can have more people show up. His theory is that it will create more opportunities for conversation because we're all in the same place, but some people don't like it. Imagine if you don't want to hook up, and people keep hitting on you. Tonight, there are two singles meetups—one for the twenties and thirties and one for the forties and fifties—plus the new-to-town meetup," Philip explains.

"That makes sense," I say. As I look around the room, I notice that the brunette is now standing behind us in line, waiting for drinks too.

I turn back to Phillip.

"You'd be surprised," Philip continues, shrugging his shoulders and motioning toward the bartender. "This place inspires a lot of conversation."

"A room full of new people to meet," I say, turning back toward the brunette in line behind me. Flashing a smile, I continue, "At the end of the day, we're all here socializing and looking to meet new people."

"I agree," she responds. "What's your name? I'm Kierra."

"Joel Edmonds," I say, and we shake hands. "I'm new to the city, just moved here a couple of weeks ago. This is Phillip," I say, motioning toward my new friend, who is in the process of paying the bartender for our next round of drinks. "We met a little bit earlier tonight," I say.

"This is Kailani," Kierra says, introducing her friend. "We met a few weeks ago." I smile and nod. She extends her hand, and we shake.

"Hi," she says with a smile.

"A pleasure to meet you," I respond.

"I couldn't help but overhear what you said about Mike's events. It's like, we're out being social, and this is The Connect Lounge. Who cares if it's the singles meetup or a new-to-town? I'm glad we're all here," Kierra says with a beautiful smile.

I smile and nod. "Are you from around here?"

"I've been here for a couple of months now," Kierra says. "I moved from Minnesota."

"Really? I just moved here from Des Moines," I say. "What brings you to town?"

"I got a senior financial analyst position at a company called Daintree," she says, smiling and glancing at Kailani.

"I remember you from a couple of weeks ago over at the meetup in Ballard," Philip chimes in, handing me my drink. "Check it out. At the distillery, right?"

"Yeah," Kierra says, making the connection, snapping her fingers and pointing at Phillip. "I won two tickets to the T-Bird's game at that meetup's drawing. I had a lot of fun."

"Nice," Philip says. "How was that?"

"It was last week," she says with bright eyes and a big smile. "It was fun. I took Kailani."

"Yeah, there were cowbells and all kinds of fights and stuff," Kailani says with a grin as she mimics throwing punches. "It was awesome."

I raise my eyebrows, looking at Philip. My heart begins racing.

"It was a lot more aggressive than I was anticipating," Kierra says.

"There's a junior hockey league out here?" I ask.

"Oh yeah, there are a few teams," Philip says. "There are even rumors the NHL will expand here in a couple of years."

"I'm a fan too," I say to Kierra, adding to the conversation. "I had season tickets for a minor-league team, the Iowa Grizzlies."

"You had Grizzlies season tickets?" Kierra asks. "I've heard of them, but I've never been to a game. They were like four hours away by car from where I lived in Minnesota."

"Have you been to Pike Place yet?" I ask.

"I've passed by, but I haven't gone through it," Kierra says bashfully.

"Philip mentioned earlier how nice it was and suggested checking it out. Would you be interested in getting together and checking it out with me?" I ask.

"Yeah, sure," Kierra says with a smile. "How random that we're both from the Midwest and happen to relocate out here," she says, playing with her hair.

Somehow, we end up in our own conversation, and I notice Phillip in conversation with Kailani, facing the opposite direction.

"Can I have your phone number?" I ask Kierra.

"Yeah," she says, and I hand her my phone so she can enter her contact information.

* * *

Four days later, I have my final coaching call with Coach Thomas.

"Hey, Coach Thomas. How are you doing?" I ask.

"I'm well, Joel. How are you? How's Seattle?" he asks.

"I'm doing well out here. The rain isn't as bad as I was anticipating," I say.

"How nice," he continues. "How has the week been since you arrived in the city? What are you up to?"

"I feel like I've made progress, and I'm starting to realize that this is where I want to be, regardless of the challenges. I'm also clarifying my expectations about working with this store," I begin. "It's a challenge and not quite what I anticipated, but I feel like I'm in the right place, and I want this to work. I'm excited about this opportunity."

"That's so good to hear, Joel. Is there anything you want to talk about today?" Coach Thomas asks.

"There is something else I want to mention," I say.

"Yeah, what's that?" he asks.

"I met a girl last week," I begin. "We happened to be in close proximity to each other at a meetup and struck up a conversation. It turns out that she's from Minnesota and moved to town not that long ago. We're getting together this weekend at Pike Place."

"Congratulations, Joel," Coach replies. "This is good news."

"Heck yeah, I'm excited," I say. "It's been a journey getting to this point. Working with you and doing those exercises, I feel like I've been progressing my life, and I'm not the same anymore. Being in this new place and doing those exercises around who I want to be and how I want to show up—well, things have shifted for me."

"Well, Joel, you've been up to so much over there," Coach Thomas says. "So, is there anything you'd like to discuss around this transformation?"

"Transformation . . . ," I repeat. I pause and think about it. "With everything going on, from figuring out things in the territory and at the store, having some conversations to develop relationships here, and meeting Kierra, I feel quite optimistic for the future," I say.

"Would it serve you if we did an exercise to support both of us in reflecting completion around our time working together? Sometimes, moments of clarity come up for clients that support the next step of their journey as we complete this phase of working together, creating a space for what's next. How does that sound?" Coach Thomas asks.

"I never thought about what we would do to keep in touch after our calls," I say. "I guess I imagined that we would stay in touch to some degree."

"Joel, you know I'm always going to be here for you and support your journey. The work you've done and committed to in the last three months is incredible. I'm so excited because of your willingness to continue to go deeper and work on these areas of yourself. But not just work on it—you're putting into action what you've been designing to create your future," he responds.

"Thanks, Coach," I say.

"How about if we begin? The first question is this," he starts.

Question 1: What have you noticed that has shifted for you since we first met?

"Wow, so much has shifted," I begin. "From being in the store and feeling stuck to accepting that there's only so much I can control and so much I can do. I am intentional about being in action, designing what I want, and acknowledging that what I want matters. It has given me some grounding around purpose at home and work. It's helping me center myself around the person I want to be and the community I want to be a part of. Before, I felt like I didn't have that. It felt like accepting what was given was the only option."

Question 2: What accountability have you avoided?

"Accountability?" I repeat. I think about it for a moment. "You know, I think of accepting responsibility for my part in the store with Kim and how things ended. I wasn't happy there. Patricia left and Joanne transferred out of the store. I regret offending her. I didn't know what I didn't know. I was carrying on as the store manager, doing my best with what I knew and blaming it all on John and Kim. I could've taken time to build a relationship with my staff and find common ground," I say.

Question 3: What is it costing you to hold on to that?

"Hmm," I pause to think again. "There's so much I didn't enjoy and don't want to have in my future."

"Can you see what it's currently costing you in Seattle when it comes to developing relationships in the store?" Coach Thomas asks.

I tilted my head in realization. "You know, I had a disagreement a couple of days ago, and I was able to be more direct about what I wasn't happy about. I don't think I'm holding on to frustration and miscommunication the way I had been."

Question 4: What do you notice is happening in your body about the situation?

"I've got some nerves coming up," I say. "I'm not super excited to walk into the store and get into another disagreement with

Michelle, the store manager, but I've been through this before. It's just a matter of getting support from my manager, and Grant seems a lot more supportive than John was."

Question 5: What can you leave behind and no longer carry unnecessarily?

"The trip to Florida," I say. "It was supposed to be a trip of recovery, and that's what it was. Also, the stress of the store and the frustration from the divorce. I can leave behind disappointment. I felt like I was a failure, and dealing with what was going on in the store, I was totally questioning myself and my ability."

Coach Thomas takes a deep breath. "You know, we've had a great conversation about the possibility you're stepping into around relationship and this possibility you're creating in your life. I like this next question for you.

Question 6: What is the vision you've created for your future?

"Well," I begin, "starting with The Personal Development Podcast, it was cool thinking about the characteristics I want to bring forth in Seattle and who I want to be here. The vision started to form by watching Kevin and wanting to be an outside sales rep who could connect with customers in a way that no one else was. I want to have relationships inside the store and support those I work with the way Kevin supported me. I want to be the individual a store can count on to have their back when shit is going down.

"I've also been thinking about who I want to be and my confidence, resiliency, and purpose. It's starting to shift what feels important and what I want to be around. I love seeing the mountains and the water, and I love the vibe out here."

I continue, "Now that I'm in Seattle, my focus is shifting to asking myself, 'How do I set up roots in the community outside of working at Hank and Harry's?' I want to be honest about my experience and the lessons I've learned. I want to be truthful about who I am and don't want to hide what I want or feel that what I want doesn't matter.

"Grant has been very supportive and is helping me to recognize my weaknesses and blind spots, and he's connecting me to people with the experience to support my development. I appreciated seeing someone demonstrate a way to be a sales rep outside of what I'm familiar with. It was an eye-opener. My vision for the future is to have a healthy and connected network of supportive people and relationships in my life."

Question 7: Imagine seeing yourself demonstrating what you are committed to. How does that look in action for you?

"Having honest conversations with Kierra," I begin. "I want to approach this as an opportunity for a new relationship. I'm a little nervous, but I don't think it will hold me back.

"I'm leaning into things. I love being out in nature and finding unique parts of this community. Everywhere out here, there are new features to explore, and I see myself able to plug into many new places and be around new people," I say.

Question 8: What do you intend to create from this opportunity you see for yourself?

"Coach, without a doubt, the life of my dreams," I say without hesitation. "I'm creating a life of purpose and meaning and connection. A life of honesty and vulnerability. I see myself expanding my capacity of what I can be and who I want to be around."

Question 9: What are you committed to regarding this area of life?

I think about it for a moment before speaking. "I'm committed to doing the work and stepping outside my comfort zone to do my part, and I'm also committed to not carrying someone else's burden unnecessarily. I'm not letting some unspoken expectations ruin my relationships because of a lack of communication," I answer.

"I don't want to be around negative mindsets. We're all dealing with what needs to be said or working through something. Let's collaborate to move forward. Life doesn't need to be a constant battle against one another, as it felt with Angela, Kim, or John. I'm committed to bringing my heart into relationships."

Coach Thomas says, "This is the last question I have for you, Joel, and again I want to acknowledge you for showing up consistently the last several months and for doing the work. From the actions you've committed to or sought out on your own from The Personal Development Podcast, it's been incredible to witness your transformation and see your expansion and growth. I appreciate you sharing these answers and doing this work."

Question 10: Is there anything else that you need to say?

"I'm grateful that Bart introduced us and that there are people like you in this world who are willing to show up and have these conversations that are so insightful and supportive. I'm grateful I've had your support, and I've appreciated these conversations," I begin. "The journey from my cloud of confusion after my divorce and figuring out what to do next to transition . . . I had no idea what I was going to do. I didn't have experience working with a life coach, and I feel so much more energy and optimism about our work and the direction I'm heading. I mean, I'm in Seattle. I got the new job, I have Presley, and I met a girl," I say with excitement.

"Six months ago, when I left Angela, I was feeling broken and like a failure, resigned to the fact that I didn't have any say or control over the direction of my life." I start tearing up. "I can't say enough to thank you for all of your conversation and support and for challenging me. It's been a journey, Coach."

"Look at where you are, Joel," Coach Thomas says. "You created this. You're seeing what's on the other side of what was getting in the way."

"It's a new relationship with possibility, yeah," I say. "This has been such a huge support. I'll keep your contact info to reach out again."

"Joel, this vision you've created for yourself is powerful. Remember this journey and feel free to reach out," Coach Thomas continues. "May I recommend one last thing?"

"Sure, what's that?" I respond.

"Enjoy the journey. It's the best part," he says.

"Thanks, Coach. I appreciate you," I say.

"You take care of yourself," he says in closing.

"You too, Coach Thomas. Be well," I say.

"Goodbye for now," he says, and the call ends.

***

That Saturday, I'm meeting Kierra on the corner of First Avenue and Pike Street for our first date.

As soon as I get to First and Pike, I notice that it's super crowded. There are tourists weaving on and off the sidewalks, trying to figure out where they're going or where they are going to eat. Either way, they're wandering around like lost tourists. I stand just outside a flower shop and wait for Kierra. I'm excited and nervous.

"Hey, Joel! How are you doing?" Kierra says, approaching from behind me.

"I'm good," I respond. "How are you?"

"Good. It's nice out today," she says. It's partly cloudy and cool enough for a sweatshirt or a light jacket.

We walk down the sidewalk, weaving through people, and stop for some lemonade. I admire her in her long-sleeved red sweater and jeans as she orders our drinks. Her long hair is unbraided today and drapes over her left shoulder.

"I want to get something off my chest right away," I say as we continue walking. "I'm nervous to mention it, but I'm just going to say it. I'm divorced, and I hope that doesn't scare you."

"It doesn't scare me. Thank you for telling me," Kierra says, evidently OK with my confession.

"I don't know what I thought your response would be," I say. "It felt like something I wanted to share, and it's slightly uncomfortable. Part of why I came to the city is for a new experience with intention."

I get hit by an aroma that's a cross between corn dogs and some battered-and-fried fair food. It smells delicious. "Are you hungry?" I ask as we walk down the hill toward the market.

"I could go for a bite. There are lots of good options around here," Kierra says, looking around the corner.

"Let's walk around and see what's here," I suggest.

We find ourselves inside the tourist trap of visitors in cars and pedestrians looking to maneuver in the same space. We walk on the cobblestone streets with other pedestrians, many with Star City Coffee cups in their hands.

The crowds provide the perfect excuse to walk a little closer to each other. We pass fresh fish at oyster stands, and fresh fruit and vegetables are also for sale.

"It looks like they have everything here," Kierra says.

"Hmm. Look at all the truffles and pastries," I say, pointing at a small pastry shop.

As we pass a random piano set up on the corner, I notice that people don't seem to mind maneuvering around the man playing as he fills the air with an upbeat old-timey sound. It all feels like we are in the older part of the city.

We enter the market, where there are more flower stands set up with colorful bundles for sale. The many flowers in the breezeway are surrounded by shiny jewelry and more fresh fruit for sale. If I thought it smelled like paradise outside, it smells like heaven in here.

"Flowers galore," I say out loud. "How about some?"

Kierra smiles and shakes her head, declining the offer.

We look at some locally made jewelry and honey produced by a local farmer. Tourists stop in the middle of the crowded marketplace to take pictures.

I get hit by another mouthwatering aroma. "That smells delicious. Whatever that is, we need to get some of it," I say with excitement and look around.

"Look," Kierra says and pointing ahead of us. "There is a line around the corner. It's got to be good."

We get in line. The sign out front reads "Brothers Sweet Bread and Bakery." There are awards in the window, along with local newspaper clippings. It must be worth it.

A greeter guides customers through the queue to keep pace and playfully shouts instructions regarding how to order.

"Hey, look," Kierra says, pointing behind me. "There's the original Star City Coffee Shop."

I turn to look and see another extended line down the sidewalk in the opposite direction. "Oh wow. At least our line is moving quickly," I joke.

As we enter the front door to the tiny bakery, the aroma of fresh bread mixed with a sweet nuance of fruit, sugar, and something savory gets my mouth watering.

"Mmm, it smells delicious," I say.

"Yeah, this is amazing. Look at all the options," Kierra says, pointing to a full display case of freshly prepared pastries and pies.

"We're up next. What would you like?"

"I was looking at the apple pastry."

"Me too," I say and smile.

I hear, "I can help who is next," and we make our way to the open register.

"Hi. What can I get for you?" the baker's assistant asks, dressed in a white T-shirt.

"Can we have two of the apple pastries?" I say, pointing to the sweet pies with assorted fillings in the glass display case.

"Would you like anything else?" the chef asks as the assistant picks our small pies from the glowing display case.

"How about some water?" Kierra suggests.

"Sure thing," the chef says, typing on the register. "That'll be twenty-one dollars and eighty-five cents."

I pay for the pastries, and we walk to a patio overlooking the water. We find a spot with several open picnic tables set for people to eat lunch. The sky is a brilliant blue, and the red umbrellas provide shade from the sun.

We sit down to eat our pastries.

"What a beautiful view of the water," Kierra says.

"It is a beautiful view—you can see the Ferris wheel and Mount Rainier," I say. "Look, there are even a few sailboats on the water. Before I moved here, my buddy told me to expect it to be raining all the time. He has no idea about days like today."

The smell of apple and cinnamon is delicious. I cut into the buttery pastry. The flaky crust gives way like a croissant but with a soft, sweetened dough center.

"This looks delicious," Kierra says.

I take my first bite, and my mouth begins to water. "This is delicious," I say. "Green apple, *mmm*."

"Wow," Kierra says. "I'm glad we stopped at this place." Her eyes are bright while she's chewing and smiling. "Remember Brothers Sweet Bread Bakery."

Sitting by the water, we continue talking.

"I used to think, growing up, that if I let love go, it would come back to me," I say.

"How's that working out for you?" Kierra asks with a slight chuckle.

"I got tired of looking in the rearview mirror," I say, shrugging my shoulders. "When I saw you, I felt a spark, like electricity. I thought, *Where else does this show up in my life, just wanting things to happen versus leaning in and taking action?* It's been a journey to realize patterns, and I'm glad I said hi."

"I'm glad too," Kierra says nervously.

"Working with a life coach, I'm learning that mistakes and failures are not the same," I continue. "What do you truly desire in your relationships?"

After some thought, Kierra says, "Being able to step into my voice," she says. "I feel like there was a power dynamic in my last relationship back in Minnesota, and I was giving away my power. Like, we both should have valuable contributions to offer and receive. Do you know what you want in your next relationship?"

"I guess I'm starting to recognize that it comes down to trusting myself," I say. "Trusting myself to show up, be vulnerable, and be a real partner. Modeling love at a new level of trust, commitment, and compassion as part of the relationship's ongoing foundation."

"Yeah, vulnerability is so nice when other people are doing it," Kierra says.

"I want to lean into that," I say in agreement.

We get up and walk toward the corner of the market and wander slowly through the crowd. I fail to notice a large group of gathering tourists just in front of us. All I see is a fish flying through the air out of the corner of my eye, and I duck in panic.

"Oh, whoa!" I yell on the way down.

Kierra starts laughing.

We happened to be walking past the flying fish stand known for tossing fish for the crowd. As I get up, I say to Kierra, "Did you see the thing almost hit me?"

"Hey, man, did you hear us yelling?" asks the market employee.

"No, I didn't," I say. I was staring at Kierra, looking at her, and smiling embarrassingly. She is still laughing at the scene with the crowd of people around us.

"Oh my God, that's hilarious," she says through her laughter.

"You've got to watch where you're walking, man," the vendor says jokingly.

"Are you OK?" Kierra asks.

"Yeah," I chuckle. "I think I'll be OK."

She hugs me and holds my hand. My heart skips a beat again. It's been such a long time since I've felt this sense of attraction. I want to wrap my arms around her right now, but I try my best to play it cool.

As we continue walking, I begin again. "You talked about going to a hockey game not that long ago, and I haven't been in a while. Would you want to go sometime?"

"That would be awesome," she says enthusiastically.

My heart is racing because I want to kiss her, and I can see a look in her eyes that makes me feel like a magnet is pulling us together.

"I had a good time today," she says.

"Me too. Who would've known you could have an apple pastry like that," I say.

"Yeah," she says with a big smile. "Thanks for trying that with me."

"Of course," I say and step a little closer. "I'll look into getting us some hockey tickets soon."

"That'd be a lot of fun," she says, then leans in.

I close my eyes and lean in too.

Acknowledgments

To my friends and family: I wouldn't be the man I am today without your love and support. Thank you for believing in me as I continue to step into new possibilities and the unknown.

This book would not be the same story without Amanda Rooker and Split Seed Media's support over the last year and a half. Your patience, flexibility, insight, and expertise were the pillars that allowed me to find my voice and craft my story at a level beyond what I imagined possible. Your accountability and coaching support were the very motivation I needed. Your support in writing this book and referral to my coaching training program transformed the story and my life. Your belief in me held the space for me to believe in me to create this meaningful work that supports my realized life purpose. Thank you, thank you!

I want to thank the members of my coaching training cohort and leadership team for your support and feedback during our year in the program together. Your vulnerability, accountability, and openness to our relationship found my life at the right time. I respect everyone's coaching ability—thank you for demonstrating how we can create impact and support as ontological life coaches. I appreciate all of you and your friendship, and I look forward to continuing our coaching journeys together and continuing to stand for you.

I thank my coworkers for your support and leadership over the past thirteen years in retail. Our relationships mean so much to me, and

I'm grateful to have spent time on my journey with you. You've each brought something special to my life.

I thank Jesse Harless for introducing me to my writing coach and your continued contribution to my journey.

About the Author

Jeremy Stegall is a business success and life coach who empowers his clients to maximize their personal and professional potential through consistent habits of growth. His first book, *Where the Change Happens*, has reached readers in the United States, the UK, India, France, Canada, Italy, the Netherlands, and Brazil and is consistently ranked as a top seller in books on divorce on Amazon.com. Jeremy received his bachelor's degree in psychology from Iowa State University and lives in Seattle, Washington. To learn more, visit wherethechangehappens.com.

Further Resources

To continue your own journey from looking back to leaning in, consider these resources:

- Receive a one-hour complimentary coaching session (a $150 value) and begin the journey where change is possible for you today. Register at wherethechangehappens.com/freeintro. Use promo code: GRIZZLIES

- To invite Jeremy to speak at your event, please email connect@wherethechangehappens.com or visit wherethechangehappens.com/contact/.

- Thinking of bringing Where the Change Happens Coaching to your group or workplace? Reach out to Jeremy at connect@wherethechangehappens.com or by visiting wherethechangehappens.com/contact/ for more information about group coaching packages, live seminars, and webinar training.

- Read Jeremy's first book, *Where the Change Happens.* Available on Amazon.

- Read Jeremy's blog on his journey of transformation and self-discovery and learn more about coaching with Jeremy and Where the Change Happens Coaching at WheretheChangeHappens.com.